"Teal shook his head, blinked the fog from before his eyes; avidly he scanned the panel.

"Nothing had changed. The instruments still gave their dataless readings; the screen was blank.

"Teal felt a sudden constriction, like a rope around his throat, as he stared at the motionless figure in the other chair.

" 'Jake!' he shouted. 'You can't be dead! Not yet! I'd be stuck here! Jake! Wake up! Wake up!' As from a great distance, he heard his own voice screaming; but he was powerless to stop it...."

—from "Mind Out of Time"
by Keith Laumer

The Farthest Reaches
was originally published by
Trident Press.

THE FARTHEST REACHES

Edited
by
JOSEPH ELDER

PUBLISHED BY POCKET BOOKS NEW YORK

THE FARTHEST REACHES

Trident Press edition published August, 1968

A *Pocket Book* edition
1st printing......September, 1969

This *Pocket Book* edition includes every word
contained in the original, higher-priced edition. It is printed
from brand-new plates made from completely reset, clear, easy-to-read
type. *Pocket Book* editions are published by Pocket Books, a division
of Simon & Schuster, Inc., 630 Fifth Avenue, New York, N.Y. 10020.
Trademarks registered in the United States and other countries.

L

For Barbara

Foreword

What we really seek in space is not knowledge, but wonder, beauty, romance, novelty —and above all, adventure. Let no one devalue these by fatuous charges of "escapism"; they are essential to man because of his very nature.

Arthur C. Clarke, one of the distinguished contributors to this collection, addressed these words to The Fifth Goddard Memorial Symposium of the American Astronautical Society in the spring of 1967. Three cheers and one cheer more for Arthur C. Clarke! His words struck a responsive chord in me as I assembled these stories, for they expressed precisely the theme I had hoped to capture in this book. We hear enough about the uses of space: space for research, space for peace, space for war, space for commerce and industry, etc. What about space for the soul?

This, to my way of thinking, is what science fiction is all about. It may be firmly rooted in scientific fact and reality. Occasionally, it comes up with some startling predictions which, in time, are proved accurate. On the other hand, it is frequently (indeed, more often) far off the mark, or it doesn't even pretend to have anything to do with the world of "real" science. We didn't need *Mariner V* to prove that Ray Bradbury's Mars of *The Martian Chronicles* bears no resemblance to the realities of our neighboring planet; but if Bradbury's isn't one of the great works of science fiction, I'll eat my space helmet. It endures, as does all great science fiction, because it embodies to an extraordinary degree the very wonder, beauty, romance, novelty, and adventure to which Mr. Clarke referred in his address. In essence, science fiction may have very little to do with science.

Escapism? Of course. Science fiction is just that, and, as such, it opens infinite doors to adventure, exploration, and ways of life totally alien to our own. It creates whole new worlds of imagination in a way that no other form of fiction can. Does it need any other raison d'être? In my belief, no.

There are those who claim mainstream status for the genre, those who feel that it can and sometimes does equal the best of what the straight fiction boys are doing. I hope I do not offend my good contributors by taking an opposing point of view. What science fiction do we have to rival Dickens or Tolstoi or Kazantzakis? Will there ever be science fiction to compete with the masterworks of literature? It seems to me extremely doubtful, though not impossible (to the SF fan, *nothing* is impossible) that there will be, for the simple reason that science fiction, by its very nature, is and always will be a *category*, a tributary of the mainstream, in the same way that western fiction, for example, is saddled (pun fully intended) by *its* own nature. The reader, and indeed the writer, of the western is excited by cowboys and Indians, blazing sixguns, the beckoning spaces of the frontier, the strange ways of the redman. Whether he admits it or not, the diehard science-fiction fan, and writer, is excited by spacemen and bug-eyed monsters, blazing ray guns, the awesomeness of infinity, the wonder of limitless life forms in the universe.

The parallels are close and obvious. In neither western nor science fiction, however, does one find the ultimate communication between mind and mind, between heart and heart, or confront the deepest truths of human feelings and relationships as one does in the great works of mainstream fiction. To be sure, the western has its occasional A. B. Guthrie, and science fiction its rare Bradbury, and they are very good indeed; but we have yet to produce our Proust of the prairie, our Stendhal of the starways. The comparison admittedly may be unfair, for of course the mainstream novel has had a long head start on western and science fiction as recognized genres of literature. A Ph.D. scholar, unearthing (perhaps literally) these words a century hence, may ridicule them as a Nobel Prize is handed out to some as yet unborn practitioner in either category. One hopes so.

It seems more likely, however, that both western and science fiction will be things of the past in another hundred years or so. (Though not the mystery novel: Crime, alas, will always be with us.) As we escape farther in time from our frontier heritage, and our landscape is further eroded, polluted, and submerged in the spreading megalopolis, and the Indian is at last no longer isolated on his reservation, who will be left to sing of sagebrush and sixgun? Our western lore will be tainted by quaintness. We will know of it only from writings of the past, and great literature is nurtured not by lesser literature, but by life.

Science fiction? It will no longer be fiction when we have colonized the solar system and set foot on those now seemingly inaccessible planets orbiting the distant stars. Something *like* science fiction may replace the genre as we know it, but it will be more akin to our present western than science fiction. It will be based not on speculation about what we may encounter in space, but on the reality of what we *have* encountered (and that will be stranger than anything dreamed of in our philosophy). The fictional settlers will be fighting for survival, not against duststorms and Indians, but perhaps against the methane storms and ammonia-breathing natives of Jupiter. An Earth hungry for the romance and adventure of space, which most of its half-starving billions of inhabitants will never hope to know firsthand, will demand and thus create this new category of space fiction. Science fiction as we know it will be one with the auk and the dodo, a victim of man's inexorable trek to the stars.

Although I shall not be there to mourn its passing, I regret it even now. One need not make excuses for science fiction. It is sufficient unto itself, and I am thankful that I am here and now able to enjoy it for what it is. (I suspect the above postulated space fiction will be about as thrilling as the last Audie Murphy movie.) Science fiction, it seems to me, is capable of lifting the reader from a humdrum world and stirring in him a sense of wonder, which he had perhaps forgotten how to feel, as no other kind of fiction can. The mystery story may have somewhat the same effect, but it is a question of degree. Be the weapon a blunt .45 or a subtle draught of poison, it remains a simple, recognizable, prosaic instrument of death not to be compared with those blazing ray guns. A body dumped from the Orient Express is a body is a body is a body, but, ah, those scaly aliens blasted from their spaceship on the Alpha Centauri run! The aliens are a bit more sophisticated these days (they even looked like us on a popular television show), but aliens are—well, alien, and mysterious in ways that no human fictional character, neither Fu Manchu nor wily redskin, can be.

Whatever its degree of sophistication, science fiction has happily never lost its sense of wonder, and that is precisely what I have tried to demonstrate in this invitational collection. The authors were asked to contribute stories set only in the farthest reaches of space beyond our solar system, in unimaginably distant galaxies; stories which reflect all those qualities which Mr. Clarke so rightly claimed as our true goals in space. Whether or not they have met their challenge I leave to the reader (I am bored and exasperated by glowing introductions written by editors who selected the very stories they are introducing), but I do make at least one immodest claim for the collection: it will not soon become dated.

Joseph Elder
Ardsley, New York 1967

Contents

Foreword   vii

The Worm That Flies
.... *Brian W. Aldiss*   *1*

Kyrie
.... *Poul Anderson*   21

Tomorrow Is a Million Years
.... *J. G. Ballard*   35

Pond Water
.... *John Brunner*   49

The Dance of the Changer
and the Three
.... *Terry Carr*   63

Crusade
.... *Arthur C. Clarke*   79

Ranging
.... *John Jakes* 85

Mind Out of Time
.... *Keith Laumer* 101

The Inspector
.... *James McKimmey* 117

To the Dark Star
.... *Robert Silverberg* 137

A Night in Elf Hill
.... *Norman Spinrad* 149

Sulwen's Planet
.... *Jack Vance* 163

The Farthest Reaches

The Worm
That Flies

by Brian W. Aldiss

When the snow began to fall, the traveler was too absorbed in his reveries to notice. He walked slowly, his stiff and elaborate garments, fold over fold, ornament over ornament, standing out from his body like a wizard's tent.

The road along which he walked had been falling into a great valley, and was increasingly hemmed in by walls of mountain. On several occasions it had seemed that a way out of these huge accumulations of earth matter could not be found, that the geological puzzle was insoluble, the chthonian arrangement of discord irresolvable: And then vale and drumlin created between them a new direction, a surprise, an escape, and the way took fresh heart and plunged recklessly still deeper into the encompassing upheaval.

The traveler, whose name to his wife was Tapmar and to the rest of the world Argustal, followed this natural harmony in complete paraesthesia, so close was he in spirit to the atmosphere presiding here. So strong was this bond, that the freak snowfall merely heightened his rapport.

Though the hour was only midday, the sky became the intense blue-gray of dusk. The Forces were nesting in the sun again, obscuring its light. Consequently, Argustal was scarce-

1

ly able to detect when the layered and fractured bulwark of rock on his left side, the top of which stood unseen perhaps a mile above his head, became patched by artificial means, and he entered the domain of the Tree-men of Or.

As the way made another turn, he saw a wayfarer before him, heading in his direction. It was a great pine, immobile until warmth entered the world again and sap stirred enough in its wooden sinews for it to progress slowly forward once more. He brushed by its green skirts, apologetic but not speaking.

This encounter was sufficient to raise his consciousness above its trance level. His extended mind, which had reached out to embrace the splendid terrestrial discord hereabouts, now shrank to concentrate again on the particularities of his situation, and he saw that he had arrived at Or.

The way bisected itself, unable to choose between two equally unpromising ravines; Argustal saw a group of humans standing statuesque in the left-hand fork. He went toward them, and stood there silent until they should recognize his presence. Behind him, the wet snow crept into his footprints.

These humans were well advanced into the New Form, even as Argustal had been warned they would be. There were five of them standing here, their great brachial extensions bearing some tender brownish foliage, and one of them attenuated to a height of almost twenty feet. The snow lodged in their branches and in their hair.

Argustal waited for a long span of time, until he judged the afternoon to be well advanced, before growing impatient. Putting his hands to his mouth, he shouted fiercely at them, "Ho then, Tree-men of Or, wake you from your arboreal sleep and converse with me. My name is Argustal to the world, and I travel to my home in far Talembil, where the seas run pink with the spring plankton. I need from you a component for my parapatterner, so rustle yourselves and speak, I beg!"

Now the snow had gone; a scorching rain had driven away its traces. The sun shone again, but its disfigured eye never looked down into the bottom of this ravine. One of the humans shook a branch, scattering water drops all around, and made preparation for speech.

This was a small human, no more than ten feet high, and the old primate form which it had begun to abandon, perhaps

2

a couple of million years ago, was still in evidence. Among the gnarls and whorls of its naked flesh, its mouth was discernible; this it opened and said, "We speak to you, Argustal-to-the-world. You are the first ape-human to fare this way in a great time. Thus you are welcome, although you interrupt our search for new ideas."

"Have you found any new ideas?" Argustal asked, with his customary boldness. "I heard there were none on all Yzazys."

"Indeed. But it is better for our senior to tell you of them, if he so judges good."

It was by no means clear to Argustal whether he wished to hear what the new ideas were, for the Tree-men were known for their deviations into incomprehensibility. But there was a minor furore among the five, as if private winds stirred in their branches, and he settled himself on a boulder, preparing to wait. His own quest was so important that all impediments to its fulfillment seemed negligible.

Hunger overtook him before the senior spoke. He hunted about and caught slow-galloping grubs under logs, and snatched a brace of tiny fish from the stream, and a handful of nuts from a bush that grew by the stream.

Night fell before the senior spoke. As he raspingly cleared his gnarled throat, one faded star lit in the sky. That was Hrt, the flaming stone. It and Yzazys' sun burned alone on the very brink of the cataract of fire that was the universe. All the rest of the night sky in this hemisphere was filled with the unlimited terror of vacancy, a towering nothingness that continued without end or beginning.

Hrt had no worlds attending it. It was the last thing in the universe. And, by the way its light flickered, the denizens of Yzazys knew that it was already infested by the Forces which had swarmed outward from their eyries in the heart of the dying galaxy.

The eye of Hrt winked many times in the empty skull of space before the senior of the Tree-men of Or wound himself up to address Argustal.

Tall and knotty, his vocal chords were clamped within his gnarled body, and he spoke by curving his branches until his finest twigs, set against his mouth, could be blown through, to give a slender and whispering version of language. The gesture made him seem curiously like a maiden who spoke with her finger cautiously to her lips.

"Indeed we have a new idea, oh, Argustal-to-the-world, though it may be beyond your grasping or our expressing. We have perceived that there is a dimension called time, and from this we have drawn a deduction.

"We will explain dimensional time simply to you like this. We know that all things have lived so long on Yzazys that their origins are forgotten. What we can remember carries from that lost-in-the-mist thing up to this present moment; it is the time we inhabit, and we are used to thinking of it as all the time there is. But we men of Or have reasoned that this is not so."

"There must be other past times in the lost distances of time," said Argustal, "but they are nothing to us because we cannot touch them as we can our own pasts."

As if this remark had never been, the silvery whisper continued, "As one mountain looks small when viewed from another, so the things that we remember in our past look small from the present. But suppose we moved back to that past to look at this present! We could not see it—yet we know it exists. And from this we reason that there is still more time in the future, although we cannot see it."

For a long while, the night was allowed to exist in silence, and then Argustal said, "Well, I don't see that as being very wonderful reasoning. We know that, if the Forces permit, the sun will shine again tomorrow, don't we?"

The small Tree-man who had first spoken said, "But 'tomorrow' is expressional time. We have discovered that tomorrow exists in dimensional time also. It is real already, as real as yesterday."

"Holy spirits!" thought Argustal to himself, "why did I get myself involved in philosophy?" Aloud he said, "Tell me of the deduction you have drawn from this."

Again the silence, until the senior drew his branches together and whispered from a bower of twiggy fingers, "We have proved that tomorrow is no surprise. It is as unaltered as today or yesterday, merely another yard of the path of time. But we comprehend that things change, don't we? You comprehend that, don't you?"

"Of course. You yourselves are changing, are you not?"

4

"It is as you say, although we no longer recall what we were before, for that thing is become too small back in time. So: if time is all of the same quality, then it has no change, and thus cannot force change. So: there is another unknown element in the world that forces change!"

Thus in their fragmentary whispers they reintroduced sin into the world.

Because of the darkness, a need for sleep was induced in Argustal. With the senior Tree-man's permission, he climbed up into his branches and remained fast asleep until dawn returned to the fragment of sky above the mountains and filtered down to their retreat. Argustal swung to the ground, removed his outer garments, and performed his customary exercises. Then he spoke to the five beings again, telling them of his parapatterner, and asked for certain stones.

Although it was doubtful whether they understood what he was about, they gave him permission, and he moved round about the area, searching for a necessary stone; his senses blowing into nooks and crannies for it like a breeze.

The ravine was blocked at its far end by a rock fall, but the stream managed to pour through the interstices of the detritus into a yet lower defile. Climbing painfully, Argustal scrambled over the mass of broken rock to find himself in a cold and moist passage, a mere cavity between two great thighs of mountain. Here the light was dim, and the sky could hardly be seen, so far did the rocks overhang on the many shelves of strata overhead. But Argustal scarcely looked up. He followed the stream where it flowed into the rock itself, to vanish forever from human view.

He had been so long at his business, trained himself over so many millennia, that the stones almost spoke to him. And he became more certain than ever that he would find a stone to fit in with his grand design.

It was there. It lay just above the water, the upper part of it polished. When he had prized it out from the surrounding pebbles and gravel, he lifted it and could see that underneath it was slightly jagged, as if a smooth gum grew black teeth. He was surprised, but as he squatted to examine it, he began to see that what was necessary to the design of his parapatterner was precisely some such roughness. At once, the next step of the design revealed itself, and he saw for the first time the whole thing as it would be in its entirety. The vision disturbed and excited him.

He sat where he was, his blunt fingers around the rough-smooth stone, and for some reason he began to think about his wife Pamitar. Warm feelings of love ran through him, so that he smiled to himself and twitched his brows.

By the time he stood up and climbed out of the defile, he knew much about the new stone. His nose-for-stones sniffed it back to times when it was a much larger affair, when it occupied a grand position on a mountain, when it was engulfed in the bowels of the mountain, when it had been cast up and shattered down, when it had been a component of a bed of rock, when that rock had been ooze, when it had been a gentle rain of volcanic sediment, showering through an unbreathable atmosphere and filtering down through warm seas in an early and unknown place.

With tender respect, he tucked the stone away in a large pocket and scrambled back along the way he had come. He made no farewell to the five of Or. They stood mute together, branch-limbs interlocked, dreaming of the dark sin of change.

Now he made haste for home, traveling first through the borderlands of Old Crotheria and then through the region of Tamia, where there was only mud. Legends had it that Tamia had once known fertility, and that speckled fish had swum in streams between forests; but now mud conquered everything, and the few villages were of baked mud, while the roads were dried mud, the sky was the color of mud, and the few mud-colored humans, who chose for their own mud-stained reasons to live here, had scarcely any antlers growing from their shoulders and seemed about to deliquesce into mud. There wasn't a decent stone anywhere about the place. Argustal met a tree called David-by-the-moat-that-dries that was moving into his own home region. Depressed by the everlasting brownness of Tamia he begged a ride from it, and climbed into its branches. It was old and gnarled, its branches and roots equally hunched, and it spoke in grating syllables of its few ambitions.

As he listened, taking pains to recall each syllable while he waited long for the next, Argustal saw that David spoke by much the same means as the people of Or had done, stuffing whistling twigs to an orifice in its trunk; but whereas it seemed that the Tree-men were losing the use of their vocal chords, the man-tree was developing some from the stringy integuments of its fibers, so that it became a nice problem as to which was inspired by which, which copied which, or whether —for both sides seemed so self-absorbed that this also was a possibility—they had come on a mirror-image of perversity independently.

"Motion is the prime beauty," said David-by-the-moat-that-dries, and took many degrees of the sun across the muddy sky to say it. "Motion is in me. There is no motion in the ground. In the ground there is not motion. All that the ground contains is without motion. The ground lies in quiet and to lie in the ground is not to be. Beauty is not in the ground. Beyond the ground is the air. Air and ground make all there is and I would be of the ground and air. I was of the ground and of the air but I will be of the air alone. If there is ground, there is another ground. The leaves fly in the air and my longing goes with them but they are only part of me because I am of wood. Oh, Argustal, you know not the pains of wood!"

Argustal did not indeed, for long before this gnarled speech was spent, the moon had risen and the silent muddy night had fallen with Hrt flickering overhead, and he was curled asleep in David's distorted branches, the stone in his deep pocket.

Twice more he slept, twice more watched their painful progress along the unswept tracks, twice more joined converse with the melancholy tree—and when he woke again, all the heavens were stacked with fleecy clouds that showed blue between, and low hills lay ahead. He jumped down. Grass grew here. Pebbles littered the track. He howled and shouted with pleasure. The mud had gone.

Crying his thanks, he set off across the heath.

". . . growth . . . ," said David-by-the-moat-that-dries.

The heath collapsed and gave way to sand, fringed by sharp grass that scythed at Argustal's skirts as he went by. He ploughed across the sand. This was his own country, and he rejoiced, taking his bearing from the occasional cairn that pointed a finger of shade across the sand. Once one of the Forces flew over, so that for a moment of terror the world was plunged in night, thunder growled, and a paltry hundred drops of rain spattered down; then it was already on the far confines of the sun's domain, plunging away—no matter where!

Few animals, fewer birds, still survived. In the sweet deserts of Outer Talembil, they were especially rare. Yet Argustal passed a bird sitting on a cairn, its hooded eye bleared with a million years of danger. It clattered one wing at sight of him, in tribute to old reflexes, but he respected the hunger in his belly too much to try to dine on sinews and feathers, and the bird appeared to recognize the fact.

He was nearing home. The memory of Pamitar was sharp before him, so that he could follow it like a scent. He passed another of his kind, an old ape wearing a red mask hanging almost to the ground; they barely gave each other a nod of recognition. Soon on the idle skyline he saw the blocks that marked Gornilo, the first town of Talembil.

The ulcerated sun traveled across the sky. Stoically, Argustal traveled across the intervening dunes, and arrived in the shadow of the white blocks of Gornilo.

No one could recollect now—recollection was one of the lost things that many felt privileged to lose—what factors had determined certain features of Gornilo's architecture. This was an ape-human town, and perhaps in order to construct a memorial to yet more distant and dreadful things, the first inhabitants of the town had made slaves of themselves and of the other creatures that were now no more, and erected these great cubes that now showed signs of weathering, as if they tired at last of swinging their shadows every day about their bases. The ape-humans who lived here were the same ape-humans who had always lived here; they sat as untiringly under their mighty memorial blocks as they had always done— calling now to Argustal as he passed as languidly as one flicks stones across the surface of a lake—but they could recollect no longer if or how they had shifted the blocks across the desert; it might be that that forgetfulness formed an integral part of being as permanent as the granite of the blocks.

Beyond the blocks stood the town. Some of the trees here were visitors, bent on becoming as David-by-the-moat-that-dries was, but most grew in the old way, content with ground and indifferent to motion. They knotted their branches this way and slatted their twigs that way, and humped their trunks the other way, and thus schemed up ingenious and ever-changing homes for the tree-going inhabitants of Gornilo.

At last Argustal came to his home, on the far side of the town.

The name of his home was Cormok. He pawed and patted and licked it first before running lightly up its trunk to the living room.

Pamitar was not there.

He was not surprised at this, hardly even disappointed, so serene was his mood. He walked slowly about the room, sometimes swinging up to the ceiling in order to view it better, licking and sniffing as he went, chasing the after-images of his wife's presence. Finally, he laughed and fell into the middle of the floor.

"Settle down, boy!" he said.

Sitting where he had dropped, he unloaded his pockets, taking out the five stones he had acquired in his travels and laying them aside from his other possessions. Still sitting, he disrobed, enjoying doing it inefficiently. Then he climbed into the sand bath.

While Argustal lay there, a great howling wind sprang up, and in a moment the room was plunged into sickly grayness. A prayer went up outside, a prayer flung by the people at the unheeding Forces not to destroy the sun. His lower lip moved in a gesture at once of contentment and contempt; he had forgotten the prayers of Talembil. This was a religious city. Many of the Unclassified congregated here from the waste miles, people or animals whose minds had dragged them aslant from what they were into rococo forms that more exactly defined their inherent qualities, until more they resembled forgotten or extinct forms, or forms that had no being till now, and acknowledged no common cause with any other living thing—except in this desire to preserve the festering sunlight from further ruin.

Under the fragrant grains of the bath, submerged all but for head and a knee and hand, Argustal opened wide his perceptions to all that might come: And finally thought only what he had often thought while lying there—for the armories of cerebration had long since been emptied of all new ammunition, whatever the Tree-men of Or might claim—that in such baths, under such an unpredictable wind, the major

Brian W. Aldiss

life forms of Yzazys, men and trees, had probably first come at their impetus to change. But change itself . . . had there been a much older thing blowing about the world that everyone had forgotten?

For some reason, that question aroused discomfort in him. He felt dimly that there was another side of life than contentment and happiness; all beings felt contentment and happiness; but were those qualities a unity, or were they not perhaps one side only of a—of a shield?

He growled. Start thinking gibberish like that and you ended up human with antlers on your shoulders!

Brushing off the sand, he climbed from the bath, moving more swiftly than he had done in countless time, sliding out of his home, down to the ground, without bothering to put on his clothes.

He knew where to find Pamitar. She would be beyond the town, guarding the parapatterner from the tattered angry beggars of Talembil.

The cold wind blew, with an occasional slushy thing in it that made a being blink and wonder about going on. As he strode through the green and swishing heart of Gornilo, treading among the howlers who knelt casually everywhere in rude prayer, Argustal looked up at the sun. It was visible by fragments, torn through tree and cloud. Its face was blotched and pimpled, sometimes obscured altogether for an instant at a time, then blazing forth again. It sparked like a blazing blind eye. A wind seemed to blow from it that blistered the skin and chilled the blood.

So Argustal came to his own patch of land, clear of the green town, out in the stirring desert, and his wife Pamitar, to the rest of the world called Miram. She squatted with her back to the wind, the sharply flying grains of sand cutting about her hairy ankles. A few paces away, one of the beggars pranced among Argustal's stones.

Pamitar stood up slowly, removing the head shawl from her head.

"Tapmar!" she said.

Into his arms he wrapped her, burying his face in her shoulder. They chirped and clucked at each other, so en-

10

grossed that they made no note of when the breeze died and the desert lost its motion and the sun's light improved.

When she felt him tense, she held him more loosely. At a hidden signal, he jumped away from her, jumping almost over her shoulder, springing ragingly forth, bowling over the lurking beggar into the sand.

The creature sprawled, two-sided and misshapen, extra arms growing from arms, head like a wolf, back legs bowed like a gorilla, clothed in a hundred textures, yet not unlovely. It laughed as it rolled and called in a high clucking voice, "Three men sprawling under a lilac tree and none to hear the first one say, 'Ere the crops crawl, blows fall,' and the second abed at night with mooncalves, answer me what's the name of the third, feller?"

"Be off with you, you mad old crow!"

And as the old crow ran away, it called out its answer, laughing, "Why Tapmar, for he talks to nowhere!" confusing the words as it tumbled over the dunes and made its escape.

Argustal and Pamitar turned back to each other, vying with the strong sunlight to search out each other's faces, for both had forgotten when they were last together, so long was time, so dim was memory. But there were memories, and as he searched they came back. The flatness of her nose, the softness of her nostrils, the roundness of her eyes and their brownness, the curve of the rim of her lips: All these, because they were dear, became remembered, thus taking on more than beauty.

They talked gently to each other, all the while looking. And slowly something of that other thing he suspected on the dark side of the shield entered him—for her beloved countenance was not as it had been. Around her eyes, particularly under them, were shadows and faint lines creased from the sides of her mouth. In her stance too, did not the lines flow more downward than heretofore?

The discomfort growing too great, he was forced to speak to Pamitar of these things, but there was no proper way to express them. She seemed not to understand, unless she understood and did not know it, for her manner grew agitated, so that he soon forwent questioning, and turned to the parapatterner to hide his unease.

It stretched over a mile of sand, and rose several feet into the air. From each of his long expeditions, he brought back no more than five stones, yet there were assembled here many hundreds of thousands of stones, perhaps millions, all painstakingly arranged, so that no being could take in the arrangement from any one position, not even Argustal. Many were supported in the air at various heights by stakes or poles, more lay on the ground, where Pamitar always kept the dust and the wild men from encroaching them; and of these on the ground, some stood isolated, while others lay in profusion, but all in a pattern that was ever apparent only to Argustal—and he feared that it would take him until the next sunset to have that pattern clear in his head again. Yet already it started to come clearer, and he recalled with wonder the devious and fugal course he had taken, walking down to the ravine of the Tree-men of Or, and knew that he still contained the skill to place the new stones he had brought within the general pattern with reference to that natural harmony—so completing the parapatterner.

And the lines on his wife's face: Would they too have a place within the pattern?

Was there sense in what the crow beggar had cried, that he talked to nowhere? And . . . and . . . the terrible and, would nowhere answer him?

Bowed, he took his wife's arm, and scurried back with her to their home high in the leafless tree.

"My Tapmar," she said that evening as they ate a dish of fruit, "it is good that you come back to Gornilo, for the town sedges up with dreams like an old river bed, and I am afraid."

At this he was secretly alarmed, for the figure of speech she used seemed to him an apt one for the newly observed lines on her face; so that he asked her what the dreams were in a voice more timid than he meant to use.

Looking at him strangely, she said, "The dreams are as thick as fur, so thick that they congeal my throat to tell you of them. Last night, I dreamed I walked in a landscape that seemed to be clad in fur all around the distant horizons, fur that branched and sprouted and had somber tones of russet and dun and black and a lustrous black-blue. I tried to resolve this strange material into the more familiar shapes of hedges and old distorted trees, but it stayed as it was, and I became . . . well, I had the word in my dream that I became a *child*."

12

Argustal looked aslant over the crowded vegetation of the town and said, "These dreams may not be of Gornilo but of you only, Pamitar. What is *child?*"

"There's no such thing in reality, to my knowledge, but in the dream the child that was I was small and fresh and in its actions at once nimble and clumsy. It was alien from me, its motions and ideas ever mine—and yet it was all familiar to me. I was it, Tapmar, I was that child. And now that I wake, I become sure that I once was such a thing as a *child.*"

He tapped his fingers on his knees, shaking his head and blinking in a sudden anger. "This is your bad secret, Pamitar! I knew you had one the moment I saw you! I read it in your face which has changed in an evil way! You know you were never anything but Pamitar in all the millions of years of your life, and that *child* must be an evil phantom that possesses you. Perhaps you will now be turned into *child!*"

She cried out and hurled a green fruit into which she had bitten. Deftly, he caught it before it struck him.

They made a provisional peace before settling for sleep. That night, Argustal dreamed that he also was small and vulnerable and hardly able to manage the language; his intentions were like an arrow and his direction clear.

Waking, he sweated and trembled, for he knew that as he had been *child* in his dream, so he had been *child* once in life. And this went deeper than sickness. When his pained looks directed themselves outside, he saw the night was like shot silk, with a dappled effect of light and shadow in the dark blue dome of the sky, which signified that the Forces were making merry with the sun while it journeyed through Yzazys; and Argustal thought of his journeys across the face of Yzazys, and of his visit to Or, when the Tree-men had whispered of an unknown element that forces change.

"They prepared me for this dream!" he muttered. He knew now that change had worked in his very foundations; once, he had been this thin tiny alien thing called *child,* and his wife too, and possibly others. He thought of that little apparition again, with its spindly legs and piping voice; the horror of it chilled his heart; he broke into prolonged groans that all Pamitar's comforting took a long part of the dark to silence.

He left her sad and pale. He carried with him the stones he had gathered on his journey, the odd-shaped one from the ravine and the ones he had acquired before that. Holding them tightly to him, Argustal made his way through the town to his spatial arrangement. For so long, it had been his chief preoccupation; today, the long project would come to completion; yet because he could not even say why it had so preoccupied him, his feelings inside lay flat and wretched. Something had got to him and killed contentment.

Inside the prospects of the parapatterner, the old beggarly man lay, resting his shaggy head on a blue stone. Argustal was too low in spirit to chase him away.

"As your frame of stones will frame words, the words will come forth stones," cried the creature.

"I'll break your bones, old crow!" growled Argustal, but inwardly he wondered at this vile crow's saying and at what he had said the previous day about Argustal's talking to nowhere, for Argustal had discussed the purpose of his structure with nobody, not even Pamitar. Indeed, he had not recognized the purpose of the structure himself until two journeys back—or had it been three or four? The pattern had started simply as a pattern (hadn't it?) and only much later had the obsession become a purpose.

To place the new stones correctly took time. Wherever Argustal walked in his great framework, the old crow followed, sometimes on two legs, sometimes on four. Other personages from the town collected to stare, but none dared step inside the perimeter of the structure, so that they remained far off, like little stalks growing on the margins of Argustal's mind.

Some stones had to touch, others had to be just apart. He walked and stooped and walked, responding to the great pattern that he now knew contained a universal law. The task wrapped him around in an aesthetic daze similar to the one he had experienced traveling the labyrinthine way down to Or, but with greater intensity.

The spell was broken only when the old crow spoke from a few paces away in a voice level and unlike his usual sing-song. And the old crow said, "I remember you planting the very first of these stones here when you were a child."

Argustal straightened.

Cold took him, though the bilious sun shone bright. He

could not find his voice. As he searched for it, his gaze went across to the eyes of the beggar-man, festering in his black forehead.

"You know I was once such a phantom—a child?" he asked.

"We are all phantoms. We were all childs. As there is gravy in our bodies, our hours were once few."

"Old crow . . . you describe a different world—not ours!"

"Very true, very true. Yet that other world once was ours."

"Oh, not! Not!"

"Speak to your machine about it! Its tongue is of rock and cannot lie like mine."

He picked up a stone and flung it. "That will I do! Now get away from me!"

The stone hit the old man in his ribs. He groaned painfully and danced backward, tripped, lay full length in the sand, hopeless and shapeless.

Argustal was upon him at once.

"Old crow, forgive me! It was fear at my thoughts made me attack you—and there is a certain sort of horror in your presence!"

"And in your stone-flinging!" muttered the old man, struggling to rise.

"You know of childs! In all the millions of years that I have worked at my design, you have never spoken of this. Why not?"

"Time for all things . . . and that time now draws to a close, even on Yzazys."

They stared into each other's eyes as the old beggar slowly rose, arms and cloak spread in a way that suggested he would either fling himself on Argustal or turn in flight. Argustal did not move. Crouching with his knuckles in the sand, he said, ". . . even on Yzazys? Why do you say so?"

"You are of Yzazys! We humans are not—if I call myself human. Thousands of thousands of years before you were child, I came from the heart stars with many others. There is no life there now! The rot spreads from the center! The sparks fly from sun to sun! Even to Yzazys, the hour is come. Up the galactic chimneys the footprints drum!" Suddenly he fell to the ground, was up again, and made off in haste, limbs whirling in a way that took from him all resemblance to

15

humankind. He pushed through the line of watchers and was gone.

For a while, Argustal squatted where he was, groping through matters that dissolved as they took shape, only to grow large when he dismissed them. The storm blew through him and distorted him, like the trouble on the face of the sun. When he decided there was nothing for it but to complete the parapatterner, still he trembled with the new knowledge: Without being able to understand why, he knew the new knowledge would destroy the old world.

All now was in position, save for the odd-shaped stone from Or, which he carried firm on one shoulder, tucked between ear and hand. For the first time, he realized what a gigantic structure he had wrought. It was a businesslike stroke of insight, no sentiment involved. Argustal was now no more than a bead rolling through the vast interstices around him.

Each stone held its own temporal record as well as its spatial position; each represented different stresses, different epochs, different temperatures, materials, chemicals, moulds, intensities. Every stone together represented an anagram of Yzazys, its whole composition and continuity. The last stone was merely a focal point for the whole dynamic, and as Argustal slowly walked between the vibrant arcades, that dynamic rose to pitch.

He heard it grow. He paused. He shuffled now this way, now that. As he did so, he recognized that there was no one focal position but a myriad, depending on position and direction of the key stone.

Very softly, he said, ". . . that my fears might be verified . . ."

And all about him—but softly—came a voice in stone, stuttering before it grew clearer, as if it had long known of words but never practiced them.

"Thou . . ." Silence, then a flood of sentence.

"Thou thou art, oh, thou art worm thou art sick, rose invisible rose. In the howling storm thou art in the storm. Worm thou art found out, oh, rose thou art sick and and found out flies in the night thy bed thy thy crimson life destroy. Oh—oh, rose, thou art sick! The invisible worm, the invisible worm that flies in the night, in the howling storm, has found out—

has found out thy bed of crimson joy . . . and his dark dark secret love, his dark secret love does thy life destroy."

Argustal was already running from that place.

In Pamitar's arms he could find no comfort now. Though he huddled there, up in the encaging branches, the worm that flies worked in him. Finally, he rolled away from her and said, "Who ever heard so terrible a voice? I cannot speak again with the universe."

"You do not know it was the universe." She tried to tease him. "Why should the universe speak to little Tapmar?"

"The old crow said I spoke to nowhere. Nowhere is the universe—where the sun hides at night—where our memories hide, where our thoughts evaporate. I cannot talk with it. I must hunt out the old crow and talk to him."

"Talk no more, ask no more questions! All you discover brings you misery! Look—you will no longer regard me, your poor wife! You turn your eyes away!"

"If I stare at nothing for all succeeding eons, yet I must find out what torments us!"

In the center of Gornilo, where many of the Unclassified lived, bare wood twisted up from the ground like fossilized sack, creating caves and shelters and strange limbs on which and in which old pilgrims, otherwise without a home, might perch. Here at nightfall Argustal sought out the beggar.

The old fellow was stretched painfully beside a broken pot, clasping a woven garment across his body. He turned in his small cell, trying for escape, but Argustal had him by the throat and held him still.

"I want your knowledge, old crow!"

"Get it from the religious men—they know more than I!"

It made Argustal pause, but he slackened his grip on the other by only the smallest margin.

"Because I have you, you must speak to me. I know that knowledge is pain, but so is ignorance once one has sensed its presence. Tell me more about childs and what they did! Tell me of what you call the heart stars!"

As if in a fever, the old crow rolled about under Argustal's grip. He brought himself to say, "What I know is so little, so little, like a blade of grass in a field. And like blades of grass are the distant bygone times. Through all those times come

17

the bundles of bodies now on this Earth. Then as now, no new bodies. But once . . . even before those bygone times . . . you cannot understand . . ."

"I understand well enough."

"You are scientist! Before bygone times was another time, and then . . . then was childs and different things that are not any longer, many animals and birds and smaller things with frail wings unable to carry them over long time . . ."

"What happened? Why was there change, old crow?"

"Men . . . scientists . . . make understanding of the gravy of bodies and turn every person and thing and tree to eternal life. We now continue from that time, a long long time—so long we have forgotten what was then done."

The smell of him was like an old pie. Argustal asked him, "And why now are no childs?"

"Childs are just small adults. We are adults, having become from child. But in that great former time, before scientists were on Yzazys, adults produced childs. Animals and trees likewise. But with eternal life, this cannot be—those child-making parts of the body have less life than stone."

"Don't talk of stone! So we live forever . . . you old ragbag, you remember—ah, you remember me as child?"

But the old ragbag was working himself into a kind of fit, pummeling the ground, slobbering at the mouth.

"Seven shades of lilac, even worse I remember myself a child, running like an arrow, air, everywhere fresh rosy air. So I am mad, for I remember!" He began to scream and cry, and the outcasts round about took up the wail in chorus. "We remember, we remember!"—whether they did or not.

Clapping his hand over the beggar's mouth, Argustal said, "But you were not child on Yzazys—tell me about that!"

Shaking, the other replied, "Earlier I tell you—all humans come from heart stars. Yzazys here is perched on universe's end! Once were as many worlds as days in eternity, now all burned away as smoke up the chimney. Only this last place was safe."

"What happened? Why?"

"Nothing happened! Life is life is life—only except that change crept in."

And what was this but an echo of the words of the Tree-men of Or who, deep in their sinful glade, had muttered of some unknown element that forced change? Argustal crouched with bowed head while the beggarman shuddered beside him, and outside the holy idiots took up his last words in a chant: "Change crept in! Change crept in! Daylight smoked and change crept in! Change crept in!"

Their dreadful howling worked like spears in Argustal's flank. He had pictures afterward of his panic run through the town, of wall and trunk and ditch and road, but it was all as insubstantial at the time as the pictures afterward. When he finally fell to the ground panting, he was unaware of where he lay, and everything was nothing to him until the religious howling had died into silence.

Then he saw he lay in the middle of his great structure, his cheek against the Or stone where he had dropped it. And as his attention came to it, the great structure around him answered without his having to speak.

He was at a new focal point. The voice that sounded was new, as cool as the previous one had been choked. It blew over him in a cool wind.

"There is no amaranth on this side of the grave, oh, Argustal, no name with whatsoever emphasis of passionate love repeated that is not mute at last. Experiment X gave life for eternity to every living thing in the world, but even eternity is punctuated by release and suffers period. The old life had its childhood and its end, the new had no such logic. It found its own after many millennia, and took its cue from individual minds. What a man was, he became; what a tree, it became."

Argustal lifted his tired head from its pillow of stone. Again the voice changed pitch and trend, as if in response to his minute gesture.

"The present is a note in music. That note can no longer be sustained. You find what questions you have found, oh, Argustal, because the chord, in dropping to a lower key, rouses you from the long dream of crimson joy that was immortality. What you are finding, others also find, and you can none of you be any longer insensible to change. Even immortality must have an end. Life has passed like a long fire through the galaxy. Now it fast burns out even here, the last refuge of man!"

He stood up then, and hurled the Or stone. It flew, fell,

rolled . . . and before it stopped he had awoken a great chorus of universal voice.

All Yzazys roused, and a wind blew from the west. As he started again to move, he saw the religious men of the town were on the march, and the great sun-nesting Forces on their midnight wing, and Hrt the flaming stone wheeling overhead, and every majestic object alert as it had never been.

But Argustal walked slowly on his flat simian feet, plodding back to Pamitar. No longer would he be impatient in her arms. There, time would be all too brief.

He knew now the worm that flew and nestled in her cheek, in his cheek, in all things, even in the Tree-men of Or, even in the great impersonal Forces that despoiled the sun, even in the sacred bowels of the universe to which he had lent a temporary tongue. He knew now that back had come that Majesty that previously gave to Life its reason, the Majesty that had been away from the world for so long and yet so brief a respite, the Majesty called DEATH.

Kyrie

by Poul Anderson

On a high peak in the Lunar Carpathians stands a convent of St. Martha of Bethany. The walls are native rock; they lift dark and cragged as the mountainside itself, into a sky that is always black. As you approach from Northpole, flitting low to keep the force screens along Route Plato between you and the meteoroidal rain, you see the cross which surmounts the tower, stark athwart Earth's blue disc. No bells resound from there—not in airlessness.

You may hear them inside at the canonical hours, and throughout the crypts below where machines toil to maintain a semblance of terrestrial environment. If you linger a while you will also hear them calling to requiem mass. For it has become a tradition that prayers be offered at St. Martha's for those who have perished in space; and they are more with every passing year.

This is not the work of the sisters. They minister to the sick, the needy, the crippled, the insane, all whom space has broken and cast back. Luna is full of such, exiles because they can no longer endure Earth's pull or because it is feared they may be incubating a plague from some unknown planet or because men are so busy with their frontiers that they have no

21

time to spare for the failures. The sisters wear space suits as often as habits, are as likely to hold a medikit as a rosary.

But they are granted some time for contemplation. At night, when for half a month the sun's glare has departed, the chapel is unshuttered and stars look down through the glaze-dome to the candles. They do not wink and their light is winter cold. One of the nuns in particular is there as often as may be, praying for her own dead. And the abbess sees to it that she can be present when the yearly mass, that she endowed before she took her vows, is sung.

> *Requiem aeternam dona eis, Domine, et lux*
> *perpetua luceat eis.*
> *Kyrie eleison, Christe eleison, Kyrie eleison.*

The Supernova Sagittarii expedition comprised fifty human beings and a flame. It went the long way around from Earth orbit, stopping at Epsilon Lyrae to pick up its last member. Thence it approached its destination by stages.

This is the paradox: time and space are aspects of each other. The explosion was more than a hundred years past when noted by men on Lasthope. They were part of a generations-long effort to fathom the civilization of creatures altogether unlike us; but one night they looked up and saw a light so brilliant it cast shadows.

That wave front would reach Earth several centuries hence. By then it would be so tenuous that nothing but another bright point would appear in the sky. Meanwhile, though, a ship overleaping the space through which light must creep could track the great star's death across time.

Suitably far off, instruments recorded what had been before the outburst, incandescence collapsing upon itself after the last nuclear fuel was burned out. A jump, and they saw what happened a century ago, convulsion, storm of quanta and neutrinos, radiation equal to the massed hundred billion suns of this galaxy.

It faded, leaving an emptiness in heaven, and the *Raven* moved closer. Fifty light-years—fifty years—inward, she studied a shrinking fieriness in the midst of a fog which shone like lightning.

Twenty-five years later the central globe had dwindled

more, the nebula had expanded and dimmed. But because the distance was now so much less, everything seemed larger and brighter. The naked eye saw a dazzle too fierce to look straight at, making the constellations pale by contrast. Telescopes showed a blue-white spark in the heart of an opalescent cloud delicately filamented at the edges.

The *Raven* made ready for her final jump, to the immediate neighborhood of the supernova.

Captain Teodor Szili went on a last-minute inspection tour. The ship murmured around him, running at one gravity of acceleration to reach the desired intrinsic velocity. Power droned, regulators whickered, ventilation systems rustled. He felt the energies quiver in his bones. But metal surrounded him, blank and comfortless. Viewports gave on a dragon's hoard of stars, the ghostly arch of the Milky Way: on vacuum, cosmic rays, cold not far above absolute zero, distance beyond imagination to the nearest human hearthfire. He was about to take his people where none had ever been before, into conditions none was sure about, and that was a heavy burden on him.

He found Eloise Waggoner at her post, a cubbyhole with intercom connections directly to the command bridge. Music drew him, a triumphant serenity he did not recognize. Stopping in the doorway, he saw her seated with a small tape machine on the desk.

"What's this?" he demanded.

"Oh!" The woman (he could not think of her as a girl, though she was barely out of her teens) started. "I . . . I was waiting for the jump."

"You were to wait at the alert."

"What have I to do?" she answered less timidly than was her wont. "I mean, I'm not a crewman or a scientist."

"You are in the crew. Special communications technician."

"With Lucifer. And he likes the music. He says we come closer to oneness with it than in anything else he knows about us."

Szili arched his brows. "Oneness?"

A blush went up Eloise's thin cheeks. She stared at the deck and her hands twisted together. "Maybe that isn't the right word. Peace, harmony, unity . . . God? . . . I sense what he means, but we haven't any word that fits."

23

"Hm. Well, you are supposed to keep him happy." The skipper regarded her with a return of the distaste he had tried to suppress. She was a decent enough sort, he supposed, in her gauche and inhibited way; but her looks! Scrawny, big-footed, big-nosed, pop eyes, and stringy dust-colored hair—and, to be sure, telepaths always made him uncomfortable. She said she could only read Lucifer's mind, but was that true?

No. Don't think such things. Loneliness and otherness can come near breaking you out here, without adding suspicion of your fellows.

If Eloise Waggoner was really human, she must be some kind of mutant at the very least. Whoever could communicate thought to thought with a living vortex had to be.

"What are you playing, anyhow?" Szili asked.

"Bach. The Third Brandenburg Concerto. He, Lucifer, he doesn't care for the modern stuff. I don't either."

You wouldn't, Szili decided. Aloud: "Listen, we jump in half an hour. No telling what we'll emerge in. This is the first time anyone's been close to a recent supernova. We can only be certain of so much hard radiation that we'll be dead if the screenfields give way. Otherwise we've nothing to go on except theory. And a collapsing stellar core is so unlike anything anywhere else in the universe that I'm skeptical about how good the thory is. We can't sit daydreaming. We have to prepare."

"Yes, sir." Whispering, her voice lost its usual harshness.

He stared past her, past the ophidian eyes of meters and controls, as if he could penetrate the steel beyond and look straight into space. There, he knew, floated Lucifer.

The image grew in him: a fireball twenty meters across, shimmering white, red, gold, royal blue, flames dancing like Medusa locks, cometary tail burning for a hundred meters behind, a shiningness, a glory, a piece of hell. Not the least of what troubled him was the thought of that which paced his ship.

He hugged scientific explanations to his breast, though they were little better than guesses. In the multiple star system of Epsilon Aurigae, in the gas and energy pervading the space around, things took place which no laboratory could imitate. Ball lightning on a planet was perhaps analogous, as the formation of simple organic compounds in a primordial ocean is

24

analogous to the life which finally evolves. In Epsilon Aurigae, magnetohydrodynamics had done what chemistry did on Earth. Stable plasma vortices had appeared, had grown, had added complexity, until after millions of years they became something you must needs call an organism. It was a form of ions, nuclei, and force-fields. It metabolized electrons, nucleons, X rays; it maintained its configuration for a long lifetime; it reproduced; it thought.

But what did it think? The few telepaths who could communicate with the Aurigeans, who had first made humankind aware that the Aurigeans existed, never explained clearly. They were a queer lot themselves.

Wherefore Captain Szili said, "I want you to pass this on to him."

"Yes, sir." Eloise turned down the volume on her taper. Her eyes unfocused. Through her ears went words, and her brain (how efficient a transducer was it?) passed the meanings on out to him who loped alongside *Raven* on his own reaction drive.

"Listen, Lucifer. You have heard this often before, I know, but I want to be positive you understand in full. Your psychology must be very foreign to ours. Why did you agree to come with us? I don't know. Technician Waggoner said you were curious and adventurous. Is that the whole truth?

"No matter. In half an hour we jump. We'll come within five hundred million kilometers of the supernova. That's where your work begins. You can go where we dare not, observe what we can't, tell us more than our instruments would ever hint at. But first we have to verify we can stay in orbit around the star. This concerns you too. Dead men can't transport you home again.

"So. In order to enclose you within the jumpfield, without disrupting your body, we have to switch off the shield screens. We'll emerge in a lethal radiation zone. You must promptly retreat from the ship, because we'll start the screen generator up sixty seconds after transit. Then you must investigate the vicinity. The hazards to look for—" Szili listed them. "Those are only what we can foresee. Perhaps we'll hit other garbage we haven't predicted. If anything seems like a menace, return at once, warn us, and prepare for a jump back to here. Do you have that? Repeat."

Words jerked from Eloise. They were a correct recital; but how much was she leaving out?

"Very good." Szili hesitated. "Proceed with your concert if you like. But break it off at zero minus ten minutes and stand by."

"Yes, sir." She didn't look at him. She didn't appear to be looking anywhere in particular.

His footsteps clacked down the corridor and were lost.

—Why did he say the same things over? asked Lucifer.

"He is afraid," Eloise said.

—?—.

"I guess you don't know about fear," she said.

—Can you show me? . . . No, do not. I sense it is hurtful. You must not be hurt.

"I can't be afraid anyway, when your mind is holding mine."

(Warmth filled her. Merriment was there, playing like little flames over the surface of Father-leading-her-by-the-hand-when-she-was-just-a-child-and-they-went-out-one-summer's-day-to-pick-wildflowers; over strength and gentleness and Bach and God.) Lucifer swept around the hull in an exuberant curve. Sparks danced in his wake.

—Think flowers again. Please.

She tried.

—They are like (image, as nearly as a human brain could grasp, of fountains blossoming with gamma-ray colors in the middle of light, everywhere light). But so tiny. So brief a sweetness.

"I don't understand how you can understand," she whispered.

—You understand for me. I did not have that kind of thing to love, before you came.

"But you have so much else. I try to share it, but I'm not made to realize what a star is."

—Nor I for planets. Yet ourselves may touch.

Her cheeks burned anew. The thought rolled on, interweaving its counterpoint to the marching music. —That is why I came, do you know? For you. I am fire and air. I had not tasted the coolness of water, the patience of earth, until you showed me. You are moonlight on an ocean.

26

"No, don't," she said. "Please."

Puzzlement: —Why not? Does joy hurt? Are you not used to it?

"I, I guess that's right." She flung her head back. "No! Be damned if I'll feel sorry for myself!"

—Why should you? Have we not all reality to be in, and is it not full of suns and songs?

"Yes. To you. Teach me."

—If you in turn will teach me— The thought broke off. A contact remained, unspeaking, such as she imagined must often prevail among lovers.

She glowered at Motilal Mazundar's chocolate face, where the physicist stood in the doorway. "What do you want?"

He was surprised. "Only to see if everything is well with you, Miss Waggoner."

She bit her lip. He had tried harder than most aboard to be kind to her. "I'm sorry," she said. "I didn't mean to bark at you. Nerves."

"We are everyone on edge." He smiled. "Exciting though this venture is, it will be good to come home, correct?"

Home, she thought: four walls of an apartment above a banging city street. Books and television. She might present a paper at the next scientific meeting, but no one would invite her to the parties afterward.

Am I that horrible? she wondered. I know I'm not anything to look at, but I try to be nice and interesting. Maybe I try too hard.

—You do not with me, Lucifer said.

"You're different," she told him.

Mazundar blinked. "Beg pardon?"

"Nothing," she said in haste.

"I have wondered about an item," Mazundar said in an effort at conversation. "Presumably Lucifer will go quite near the supernova. Can you still maintain contact with him? The time dilation effect, will that not change the frequency of his thoughts too much?"

"What time dilation?" She forced a chuckle. "I'm no physicist. Only a little librarian who turned out to have a wild talent."

"You were not told? Why, I assumed everybody was. An

intense gravitational field affects time just as a high velocity does. Roughly speaking, processes take place more slowly than they do in clear space. That is why light from a massive star is somewhat reddened. And our supernova core retains almost three solar masses. Furthermore, it has acquired such a density that its attraction at the surface is, ah, incredibly high. Thus by our clocks it will take infinite time to shrink to the Schwarzschild radius; but an observer on the star itself would experience this whole shrinkage in a fairly short period."

"Schwarzschild radius? Be so good as to explain." Eloise realized that Lucifer had spoken through her.

"If I can without mathematics. You see, this mass we are to study is so great and so concentrated that no force exceeds the gravitational. Nothing can counterbalance. Therefore the process will continue until no energy can escape. The star will have vanished out of the universe. In fact, theoretically the contraction will proceed to zero volume. Of course, as I said, that will take forever as far as we are concerned. And the theory neglects quantum-mechanical considerations which come into play toward the end. Those are still not very well understood. I hope, from this expedition, to acquire more knowledge." Mazundar shrugged. "At any rate, Miss Waggoner, I was wondering if the frequency shift involved would not prevent our friend from communicating with us when he is near the star."

"I doubt that." Still Lucifer spoke, she was his instrument and never had she known how good it was to be used by one who cared. "Telepathy is not a wave phenomenon. Since it transmits instantaneously, it cannot be. Nor does it appear limited by distance. Rather, it is a resonance. Being attuned, we two may well be able to continue thus across the entire breadth of the cosmos; and I am not aware of any material phenomenon which could interfere."

"I see." Mazundar gave her a long look. "Thank you," he said uncomfortably. "Ah . . . I must get to my own station. Good luck!" He bustled off without stopping for an answer.

Eloise didn't notice. Her mind was become a torch and a song. "Lucifer!" she cried aloud. "Is that true?"

—I believe so. My entire people are telepaths, hence we

28

have more knowledge of such matters than yours do. Our experience leads us to think there is no limit.

"You can always be with me? You always will?"

—If you so wish, I am gladdened.

The comet body curvetted and danced, the brain of fire laughed low. —Yes, Eloise, I would like very much to remain with you. No one else has ever— Joy. Joy. Joy.

They named you better than they knew, Lucifer, she wanted to say, and perhaps she did. They thought it was a joke; they thought by calling you after the devil they could make you safely small like themselves. But Lucifer isn't the devil's real name. It means only Light Bearer. One Latin prayer even addresses Christ as Lucifer. Forgive me, God, I can't help remembering that. Do You mind? He isn't Christian, but I think he doesn't need to be, I think he must never have felt sin, Lucifer, Lucifer.

She sent the music soaring for as long as she was permitted.

The ship jumped. In one shift of world line parameters she crossed twenty-five light-years to destruction.

Each knew it in his own way, save for Eloise who also lived it with Lucifer.

She felt the shock and heard the outraged metal scream, she smelled the ozone and scorch and tumbled through the infinite falling that is weightlessness. Dazed, she fumbled at the intercom. Words crackled through: ". . . until blown . . . back EMF surge . . . how should I know how long to fix the blasted thing? . . . stand by, stand by . . ." Over all hooted the emergency siren.

Terror rose in her, until she gripped the crucifix around her neck and the mind of Lucifer. Then she laughed in the pride of his might.

He had whipped clear of the ship immediately on arrival. Now he floated in the same orbit. Everywhere around, the nebula filled space with unrestful rainbows. To him, *Raven* was not the metal cylinder which human eyes would have seen, but a lambence, the shield screen reflecting a whole spectrum. Ahead lay the supernova core, tiny at this remove but alight, alight.

—Have no fears (he caressed her). I comprehend. Turbu-

29

lence is extensive, so soon after the detonation. We emerged in a region where the plasma is especially dense. Unprotected for the moment before the guardian field was reestablished, your main generator outside the hull was short-circuited. But you are safe. You can make repairs. And I, I am in an ocean of energy. Never was I so alive. Come, swim these tides with me.

Captain Szili's voice yanked her back. "Waggoner! Tell that Aurigean to get busy. We've spotted a radiation source on an intercept orbit, and it may be too much for our screen." He specified coordinates. "What *is* it?"

For the first time, Eloise felt alarm in Lucifer. He curved about and streaked from the ship.

Presently his thought came to her, no less vivid. She lacked words for the terrible splendor she viewed with him: a million-kilometer ball of ionized gas where luminance blazed and electric discharges leaped, booming through the haze around the star's exposed heart. The thing could not have made any sound, for space here was still almost a vacuum by Earth's parochial standards; but she heard it thunder, and felt the fury that spat from it.

She said for him: "A mass of expelled material. It must have lost radial velocity to friction and static gradients, been drawn into a cometary orbit, held together for a while by internal potentials. As if this sun were trying yet to bring planets to birth—"

"It'll strike us before we're in shape to accelerate," Szili said, "and overload our shield. If you know any prayers, use them."

"Lucifer!" she called; for she did not want to die, when he must remain.

—I think I can deflect it enough, he told her with a grimness she had not hitherto met in him. —My own fields, to mesh with its; and free energy to drink; and an unstable configuration; yes, perhaps I can help you. But help me, Eloise. Fight by my side.

His brightness moved toward the juggernaut shape.

She felt how its chaotic electromagnetism clawed at his. She felt him tossed and torn. The pain was hers. He battled to keep his own cohesion, and the combat was hers. They locked

30

together, Aurigean and gas cloud. The forces that shaped him grappled as arms might; he poured power from his core, hauling that vast tenuous mass with him down the magnetic torrent which streamed from the sun; he gulped atoms and thrust them backward until the jet splashed across heaven.

She sat in her cubicle, lending him what will to live and prevail she could, and beat her fists bloody on the desk.

The hours brawled past.

In the end, she could scarcely catch the message that flickered out of his exhaustion: —Victory.

"Yours," she wept.

—Ours.

Through instruments, men saw the luminous death pass them by. A cheer lifted.

"Come back," Eloise begged.

—I cannot. I am too spent. We are merged, the cloud and I, and are tumbling in toward the star. (Like a hurt hand reaching forth to comfort her:) Do not be afraid for me. As we get closer, I will draw fresh strength from its glow, fresh substance from the nebula. I will need a while to spiral out against that pull. But how can I fail to come back to you, Eloise? Wait for me. Rest. Sleep.

Her shipmates led her to sickbay. Lucifer sent her dreams of fire flowers and mirth and the suns that were his home.

But she woke at last, screaming. The medic had to put her under heavy sedation.

He had not really understood what it would mean to confront something so violent that space and time themselves were twisted thereby.

His speed increased appallingly. That was in his own measure; from *Raven* they saw him fall through several days. The properties of matter were changed. He could not push hard enough or fast enough to escape.

Radiation, stripped nuclei, particles born and destroyed and born again, sleeted and shouted through him. His substance was peeled away, layer by layer. The supernova core was a white delirium before him. It shrank as he approached, ever smaller, denser, so brilliant that brilliance ceased to have meaning. Finally the gravitational forces laid their full grip upon him.

—Eloise! he shrieked in the agony of his disintegration. —Oh, Eloise, help me!

The star swallowed him up. He was stretched infinitely long, compressed infinitely thin, and vanished with it from existence.

The ship prowled the farther reaches. Much might yet be learned.

Captain Szili visited Eloise in sickbay. Physically she was recovering.

"I'd call him a man," he declared through the machine mumble, "except that's not praise enough. We weren't even his kin, and he died to save us."

She regarded him from eyes more dry than seemed natural. He could just make out her answer. "He is a man. Doesn't he have an immortal soul too?"

"Well, uh, yes, if you believe in souls, yes, I'd agree."

She shook her head. "But why can't he go to his rest?"

He glanced about for the medic and found they were alone in the narrow metal room. "What do you mean?" He made himself pat her hand. "I know, he was a good friend of yours. Still, his must have been a merciful death. Quick, clean; I wouldn't mind going out like that."

"For him . . . yes, I suppose so. It has to be. But—" She could not continue. Suddenly she covered her ears. "Stop! Please!"

Szili made soothing noises and left. In the corridor he encountered Mazundar. "How is she?" the physicist asked.

The captain scowled. "Not good. I hope she doesn't crack entirely before we can get her to a psychiatrist."

"Why, what is wrong?"

"She thinks she can hear him."

Mazundar smote fist into palm. "I hoped otherwise," he breathed.

Szili braced himself and waited.

"She does,'" Mazundar said. "Obviously she does."

"But that's impossible! He's dead!"

"Remember the time dilation," Mazundar replied. "He fell from the sky and perished swiftly, yes. But in supernova time. Not the same as ours. To us, the final stellar collapse takes an infinite number of years. And telepathy has no distance limits." The physicist started walking fast, away from that cabin. "He will always be with her."

Tomorrow Is a Million Years

by J. G. Ballard

In the evening, the time-winds would blow across the Sea of Dreams, and the silver wreck of the excursion module would loom across the jeweled sand to where Glanville lay in the pavilion by the edge of the reef. During the first week after the crash, when he could barely move his head, he had seen the images of the *Santa Maria* and the *Golden Hind* sailing toward him through the copper sand, the fading light of the sunset illuminating the ornamental casements of the high stern castles. Later, sitting up in the surgical chair, he had seen the spectral crews of these spectral ships, their dark figures watching him from the quarter decks.

Once, when he could walk again, Glanville went out onto the surface of the lake, his wife guiding his elbow as he hobbled on his stick. Two hundred yards from the module he had suddenly seen an immense ship materialize from the wreck and move through the sand toward them, its square sails lifted by the time-winds. In the cerise light Glanville recognized the two bow anchors jutting like tusks, the try-works amidships, and the whaling irons and harpoons. Judith held his arm, drawing him back to the pavilion, but Glanville knocked away her hand. Rolling slowly, the great ship crested silently

35

through the sand, its hull towering above them as if they had been watching from a skiff twenty yards off its starboard bow. As it swept by with a faint sigh of sand, the whisper of the time-winds, Glanville pointed to the three men looking down at them from the quarter-rail, the tallest with stern eyes and a face like biscuit, the second jaunty, the third ruddy and pipe-smoking.

"Can you see them?" Glanville shouted. "Starbuck, Stubb, and Flask, the mates of the *Pequod!*" Glanville pointed to the helm, where a wild-eyed old man gazed at the edge of the reef, on which he seemed collision-bent. "Ahab . . . !" he cried in warning. But the ship had reached the reef, and then in an instant faded across the clinkerlike rocks, its mizzen sail lit for a last moment by the dying light.

"The *Pequod!* My God, you could see the crew, Ishmael, and Tashtego. . . . Ahab was there, and the mates, Melville's three momentous men! Did you see them, Judith?"

His wife nodded, helping him on toward the pavilion, her frown hidden in the dusk light. Glanville knew perfectly well that she never saw the spectral ships, but nonetheless she seemed to sense that something vast and strange moved across the sand-lake out of the time-winds. For the moment she was more interested in making certain that he recovered from the long flight, and the absurd accident when the excursion module had crashed on landing.

"But why the *Pequod?*" Glanville asked, as they sat in their chairs on the veranda of the pavilion. He mopped his plump, unshaven face with a flowered handkerchief. "The *Golden Hind* and the *Santa Maria,* yes . . . ships of discovery, Drake circumnavigating the globe has a certain resemblance to ourselves half-crossing the universe, but Crusoe's ship would have been more appropriate, don't you agree?"

"Why?" Judith glanced at the sand inundating the slatted metal floor of the veranda. She filled her glass with soda from the siphon, and then played with the sparkling fluid, watching the bubbles with her severe eyes. "Because we're marooned?"

"No . . ." Irritated by his wife's reply, Glanville turned to face her. Sometimes her phlegmatic attitude annoyed him; she seemed almost to enjoy deflating his mood of optimism, however forced that might be. "What I meant was that Crusoe, like ourselves here, made a new world for himself out of the pieces of the old he brought with him. We can do the same, Judith." He paused, wondering how to reassert his physical authority, and then said with quiet emphasis: "We're not marooned."

His wife nodded, her long face expressionless. Barely moving her head, she looked up at the night sky visible beyond the edge of the awning. High above them a single point of light traversed the starless sky, its intermittent beacon punctuating its way toward the northern pole. "No, we're not marooned—not for long, anyway, with that up there. It won't be long at all before Captain Thornwald catches up with us."

Glanville stared into the bottom of his glass. Unlike his wife, he took little pleasure from the sight of the automatic emergency beacon of the control ship broadcasting their position to the universe at large. "He'll catch up with us, all right. That's the luck of the thing. Instead of having him always at our heels we'll finally be free of him forever. They won't send anyone after Thornwald."

"Perhaps not." Judith tapped the metal table. "But how do you propose to get rid of him—don't tell me you're going to be locked together in mortal combat? At the moment you can hardly move one foot after another."

Glanville smiled with an effort, ignoring the sarcasm in his wife's voice. Whatever the qualities of skill, shrewdness, and even courage of a kind that had brought them here, she still regarded him as something of an obscure joke. At times he wondered whether it would have been better to have left her behind. Alone here, on this lost world, he would have had no one to remind him of his sagging, middle-aged figure, his little indecisions and fantasies. He would have been able to sit back in front of the long sunsets and enjoy the strange poetry of the Sea of Dreams.

However, once he had disposed of Captain Thornwald she might at last take him seriously. "Don't worry, there'll be no mortal combat—we'll let the time-winds blow over him."

Undeterred, Judith said: "You'll let one of your spectral ships run him down? But perhaps he won't see them?"

Glanville gazed out at the dark grottoes of the sand-reef that fringed the northern shore of the lake two miles away. Despite its uniformity—the lake-systems covered the entire planet—the flat perspectives of the landscape fascinated him.

37

"It doesn't matter whether he sees them or not. By the way, the *Pequod* this evening . . . it's a pity you missed Ahab. They were all there, exactly as Melville described them in *Moby Dick*."

His wife stood up, as if aware that he might begin one of his rhapsodies again. She brushed away the white sand that lay like lace across the blue brocade of her gown. "I hope you're right. Perhaps you'll see the *Flying Dutchman* next."

Distracted by his thoughts, Glanville watched her tall figure move away across the gradient of the beach, following the tideline formed by the sand blown off the lake's surface. The *Flying Dutchman?* A curious remark. By coming to this remote planet they themselves would lose seven years of their lives by time dilation if they ever chose to return home, by coincidence the period that elapsed while the condemned Dutchman roved the seas. Every seven years he would come ashore, free to stay there only if he found the love of a faithful woman.

Was he himself the Dutchman? Perhaps, in a remote sense. Or Thornwald? He and Judith had met during the preliminary inquiries, incredible though it seemed there might have been something between them—it was difficult to believe that Thornwald would have pursued them this far, sacrificing all hopes of seniority and promotion, over a minor emigration infringement. The bacterial scattering might be serious on some planets, but they had restricted themselves to arid worlds on an empty edge of the universe.

Glanville looked out at the wreck of the excursion module. For a moment there was a glimmer of royals and top-gallants, as if the entire *Cutty Sark* was about to disgorge itself from the sand. This strange phenomenon, a consequence of the time-sickness brought on by the vast distances of interstellar space, had revealed itself more and more during their long flight. The farther they penetrated into deep space the greater the nostalgia of the human mind, and its eagerness to transform any man-made object, such as the spaceships in which they traveled, into their archaic forebears. Judith, for some reason, had been immune, but Glanville had seen a succession of extraordinary visions, fragments of the myths and dreams of the Earth's past, reborn out of the dead lakes and fossil seas of the alien worlds.

Judith, of course, not only lacked all imagination but felt no sense of guilt—Glanville's crime, the memory of which he had almost completely repressed, was no responsibility of hers, man and wife though they might be. Besides, the failures of which she silently accused him every day were those of character, more serious in her eyes then embezzlement, grand larceny, or even murder. It was precisely this that made possible his plan to deal for once and for all with Captain Thornwald.

Three weeks later, when Thornwald arrived, Glanville had recovered completely from the accident. From the top of the sand-reef overhanging the western edge of the lake he watched the police captain's capsule land two hundred yards from the pavilion. Judith stood under the awning on the veranda, one hand raised to ward off the dust kicked up by the retro-jets. She had never questioned Glanville's strategy for dealing with Thornwald, but now and then he noticed her glancing upward at the beacon of the control ship, as if calculating the number of days it would take Thornwald to catch up with them. Glanville was surprised by her patience—once, a week before Thornwald arrived, he almost challenged her to say whether she really believed he would be able to outwit the police captain. By a curious irony, he realized that she probably did—but if so, why did she still despise him?

As the starboard hatch of the capsule fell back Glanville stood up on the edge of the reef and began to wave with both arms. He made his way down the side of the reef, then jumped the last five feet to the lake floor and ran across to the capsule.

"Thornwald! . . . Captain, it's good to see you!"

Framed within the steel collar of his suit, the policeman's tired face looked up at Glanville through the open hatch. He stood up with an effort and accepted Glanville's hand, then climbed down onto the ground. Careful not to turn his back on Glanville, he unzipped his suit and glanced quickly at the pavilion and the wreck of the excursion module.

Glanville strolled to and fro around him. Thornwald's cautious manner, the hand near the weapon in his holster, for some reason amused him. "Captain, you made a superb landing, beautiful marksmanship—getting here at all for that matter. You saw the beacon, I suppose, but even so." When Thornwald was about to speak, Glanville rattled on: "No, of course I didn't leave it on deliberately—damn it, we actually crashed! Can you imagine it, after coming all this way, very nearly broke our necks. Luckily, Judith was all right, not a scratch on her. She'll be glad to see you, Captain."

Thornwald nodded slowly, his eyes following Glanville's pudgy, sweating figure as it roved about the capsule. A tall, stooped man with a tough, pessimistic face and all the wariness of a long-serving policeman, he seemed somehow unsettled by Glanville's manic gaiety.

Glanville pointed to the pavilion. "Come on, we'll have lunch, you must be tired out." He gestured at the sand-lake and the blank sky. "Nothing much here, I know, but it's restful. After a few days—"

"Glanville!" Thornwald stopped. Face set, he put a hand out as if to touch Glanville's shoulder. "You realize why I'm here?"

"Of course, Captain." Glanville gave him an easy smile. "For heaven's sake, stop looking so serious. I'm not going to escape. There's nowhere to go."

"As long as you realize that." Thornwald plodded forward through the top surface of fine sand, his feet placed carefully as if testing the validity of this planet with its euphoric tenant. "You can have something to eat, then we'll get ready to go back."

"If you like, Captain. Still, there's no desperate hurry. Seven years here and back, what difference will a few hours or even days make? All those whippersnappers you left behind in the Department will be Chief Commissioners now. I wouldn't be in too much of a hurry. Besides, the emigration laws may even have been changed. . . ."

Thornwald nodded dourly. Glanville was about to introduce him to Judith, standing quietly on the veranda twenty feet from him, but suddenly Thornwald stopped and glanced across the lake, as if searching for an invisible marksman hidden among the reefs.

"All right?" Glanville asked. Changing the pitch and tempo of his voice, he remarked quietly: "I call it the Sea of Dreams. We're a long way from home, Captain, remember that. There are strange visions here at sunset. Keep your back turned on them." He waved at Judith, who was watching them approach with pursed lips. "Captain Thornwald, my dear. Rescue at last."

"Of a kind." She faced Thornwald, who stood beside Glanville, as if hesitating to enter the pavilion. "I hope you feel all this is necessary, Captain. Revenge is a poor motive for justice."

Glanville cleared his throat. "Well, yes, my dear, but . . . Come on, Captain, sit down, we'll have a drink. Judith, could you . . . ?"

After a pause she nodded and went into the pavilion. Glanville made a temporizing gesture. "A difficult moment, Captain. But as you know, Judith was always rather headstrong."

Thornwald nodded, watching Glanville as the latter drew the chairs around the table. He pointed to the wreck of the excursion module. "How badly was it damaged? We'll have a look at it later."

"A waste of time, Captain. It's a complete write-off."

Thornwald scrutinized the wreck. "Even so. I'll want to decontaminate it before we leave."

"Isn't that pointless?—no one will ever come here. The whole planet is dead. Anyway, there's a good deal of fuel in the tanks; if you short a circuit with your sprays the whole thing would go up." Glanville looked around impatiently. "Where are those drinks, Judith is . . ."

He started to stand up, and found Thornwald following him to the door of the pavilion. "It's all right, Captain."

Thornwald leaned stolidly on the door. He looked down at Glanville's plump, sweating face. "Let me help you."

Glanville shrugged and beckoned him forward, but then stopped. "Captain, for heaven's sake. If I wanted to escape I wouldn't have been waiting for you here. Believe me, I haven't got a gun hidden away in a whisky bottle or something —I just don't want a scene between you and Judith."

Thornwald nodded, then waited in the doorway. When Glanville returned with the tray he went back to his seat, eyes searching the pavilion and the surrounding beach as if looking for a missing element in a puzzle. "Glanville, I have to prefer charges against you—you're aware what you face when you get back?"

Glanville shrugged. "Of course. But after all, the offense was comparatively trivial, wasn't it?" He reached for Thornwald's bulky flight suit spread across the rail. "Let me move this out of the sun. Where's Judith gone?"

As Thornwald glanced at the door of the pavilion Glanville reached down to the steel pencil in the right knee of the suit. He withdrew it from the slot, then deliberately dropped it to the metal floor. "What's this?" he asked. "A torch?" His thumb pushed back the nozzle and then moved quickly to the spring tab.

"Don't press that!" Thornwald was on his feet. "It's a radio reflector, you'll fill the place with—" He reached across the table and tried to grasp it from Glanville, then flung up his forearm to protect his face. A blinding jet of vaporized aluminum suddenly erupted from the nozzle in Glanville's hand, gushing out like a firework. Within two or three seconds its spangled cloud filled the veranda, painting the walls and ceiling. Thornwald kicked aside the table and buried his face in his hands, his hair and forehead covered with the silver paint. Glanville backed to the steps, flecks of the paint spattering his arms and chest, hosing the jet directly at the policeman. He tossed the canister onto the floor, where its last spurts gusted out into the sunlight, swept up by the convection currents like a swarm of fireflies. Head down, Glanville turned and ran toward the edge of the sand-reef fifty yards away.

Two hours later, as he crouched deep in the grottoes of the reef on the west shore of the lake, Glanville watched with amusement as Thornwald's silver-painted figure stepped out of the pavilion into the sunlight. The cloud of vapor above the pavilion had settled, and the drab gray panels of the roof and sides were now a brilliant aluminized silver, shining in the sunlight like a temple. Framed in the doorway was Judith, watching as Thornwald walked slowly toward his capsule. Apart from the two clear handprints across his face, his entire body was covered with the aluminum particles. His hair glittered in the sunlight like silver foil.

"Glanville . . . !" Thornwald's voice, slightly querulous, echoed in the galleries of the reef. The flap of his holster was open, but the weapon still lay within its sheath, and Glanville guessed that he had no intention of trying to track him through the galleries and corridors of the reef. The columns of fused sand could barely support their own weight; every few hours there would be a dull eruption as one or other of the great pillar-systems collapsed into a cloud of dust.

Grinning to himself, Glanville watched Thornwald glance back at the pavilion. Evidently intrigued by this duel between the two men, Judith had sat down on the veranda, watching like some medieval lady at a tourney.

The police captain moved toward the reef, his legs stiff and awkward, as if self-conscious of his glittering form. Chortling, Glanville scraped the sand from the curved roof over his head and rubbed it into the flecks of silver paint on his sleeves and trousers. As he drank from the flask of water he had hidden in the reef three days earlier he glanced at his watch. It was nearly three o'clock—within four hours phantoms would move across the sand-lake. He patted the parcel wrapped in gray plastic sheeting on the ledge beside him.

At seven o'clock the time-winds began to blow across the Sea of Dreams. As the sun fell away behind the western ridges, the long shadows of the sand-reefs crossed the lakefloor, dimming the quartz-veins as if closing off a maze of secret pathways. Crouched at the foot of the reef, Glanville edged along the beach, his sand-smeared figure barely visible in the darkness. Four hundred yards away Thornwald sat alone on the veranda of the pavilion, his silver figure illuminated in the last cerise rays of the sun. Watching him across the lake-bed, Glanville assumed that already the time-winds were moving toward him, carrying strange images of ships and phantom seas, perhaps of mermaids and hallucinatory monsters. Thornwald sat stiffly in his chair, one hand on the rail in front of him.

Glanville moved along the beach, picking his way between the veins of frosted quartz. As the wreck of the excursion module and the smaller capsule nearby came between himself and the pavilion he began to see the faint outlines of a low-hulled ship, a schooner or brigantine, with its sails reefed, as if waiting at anchor in some pirate lagoon. Ignoring it, Glanville crept into a shallow fault that crossed the lake, its floor some three feet below the surrounding surface. Catching his breath, he undid the parcel, then carried the object inside it

43

under one arm as he set off toward the glimmering wreck of the module.

Twenty minutes later Glanville stepped out from his vantage point behind the excursion module. Around him rode the spectral hulks of two square-sailed ships, their bows dipping through the warm sand. Intent on the pavilion ahead of him, where the silver figure of Thornwald had stood up like an electrified ghost, Glanville stepped through the translucent image of an anchor cable that curved down into the surface of the lake in front of him. Holding the object he had taken from the parcel above his head like a lantern, he walked steadily toward the pavilion.

The hulls of the ships rode silently at their anchors behind him as he reached the edge of the lake. Thirty yards away the silver paint around the pavilion speckled the sand with a sheen of false moonlight, but the remainder of the beach and lake were in a profound darkness. As he walked the last yards to the pavilion with a slow rhythmic stride, Glanville could clearly see Thornwald's tall figure pressed against the wall of the veranda, his appalled face in the shape of his own hands staring at the apparition in front of him. As Glanville reached the steps Thornwald made a passive gesture at him, one hand raised toward the pistol lying on the table.

Quickly, Glanville threw aside the object he had carried with him. He seized the pistol before Thornwald could move, then whispered, more to himself than to Thornwald: "Strange seas, Captain, I warned you . . ."

He crouched down and began to back away along the veranda, the pistol leveled at Thornwald's chest.

Then the door opened on his left. Before he could move, the translucent figure of his wife stepped from the interior of the pavilion and knocked the weapon from his hand. He turned to her angrily, then shouted at the headless specter that stepped through him and strode off toward the dark ships moored in the center of the lake.

Two hours after dawn the next morning Captain Thornwald finished his preparations for departure. In the last minutes he stood on the veranda, gazing out at the even sunlight over the empty lake as he wiped away the last traces of the aluminum paint with a solvent sponge. He looked down at the seated figure of Glanville tied to the chair by the table. Despite the events of the previous night, Glanville now seemed composed and relaxed, a trace even of humor playing about his soft mouth.

Something about this bizarre amiability made Thornwald shudder. He secured the pistol in his holster—another evening by this insane lake and he would be pointing it at his own head.

"Captain . . ." Glanville glanced at him with docile eyes, then shrugged his fat shoulders inside the ropes. "When are you going to untie these? We'll be leaving soon."

Thornwald threw the sponge onto the silver sand below the pavilion. "*I'll* be going soon, Glanville. You're staying here." When Glanville began to protest, he said: "I don't think there's much point in your leaving. As you said, you've built your own little world here."

"But . . ." Glanville searched the captain's face. "Frankly, Thornwald, I can't understand you. Why did you come here in the first place, then? Where's Judith, by the way? She's around here somewhere."

Thornwald paused, steeling himself against the name and the memory of the previous night. "Yes, she's around here, all right." As if testing some unconscious element of Glanville's memory, he said clearly: "She's in the module, as a matter of fact."

"The module?" Glanville pulled at his ropes, then squinted over his shoulder into the sunlight. "But I told her not to go there. When's she coming back?"

"She'll be back, don't worry. This evening, I imagine, when the time-winds blow, though I don't want to be here when she comes. This sea of yours has bad dreams, Glanville."

"What do you mean?"

Thornwald walked across the veranda. "Glanville, have you any idea why I'm here, why I've hunted you all this way?"

"God only knows—something to do with the emigration laws."

"Emigration laws?" Thornwald shook his head. "Any charges there would be minor." After a pause, he said: "Murder, Glanville."

Glanville looked up with real surprise. "Murder? You're out of your mind! Of whom, for heaven's sake?"

45

Thornwald patted the raw skin around his chin. The pale image of his hands still clung to his face. "Of your wife."

"Judith? But she's here, you idiot! You saw her yourself when you arrived."

"*You* saw her, Glanville. I didn't. But I realized that you'd brought her here with you when you started playing her part, using that mincing crazy voice of yours. You weren't very keen on my going out to the module. Then last night you brought something from it for me."

Thornwald walked across the veranda, averting his eyes from the wreck of the module. He remembered the insane vision he had seen the previous evening, as he sat watching for Glanville, waiting for this madman who had absconded with the body of his murdered wife. The time-winds had carried across to him the image of a spectral ship, whose rotting timbers had formed a strange portcullis in the evening sun—a dungeon-grate! Then, suddenly, he had seen a terrifying apparition walking across this sea of blood toward him, the nightmare commander of this ship of hell, a tall woman with the slow, rhythmic stride of her own requiem, "*Her locks were yellow as gold . . . the nightmare life-in-death was she, who thins man's blood with cold.*" Aghast at the sight of Judith Glanville's face on this lamia, he had barely recognized Glanville, her mad mariner, bearing her head like a wild lantern before he snatched the pistol.

Glanville flexed his shoulders against the ropes. "Captain, I don't know about Judith . . . she's not too happy here, and we've never got on with just ourselves for company. I'd like to come with you."

"I'm sorry, Glanville, there's not much point—you're in the right place here."

"But, Captain—aren't you exceeding your authority? If there is a murder charge . . ."

"Not Captain, Glanville—Commissioner. I was promoted before I left, and that gives me absolute discretion in these cases. I think this planet is remote enough, no one's likely to come here and disturb you."

He went over to Glanville and looked down at him, then took a clasp knife from his pocket and laid it on the table. "You should be able to get a hand around that if you stand up. Good-bye, Glanville, I'll leave you here in your gilded hell."

"But, Thornwald . . . Commissioner!" Glanville swung himself around in the chair. "Where's Judith? Call her."

Thornwald glanced back across the sunlight. "I can't, Glanville. But you'll see her soon. This evening, when the time-winds blow, they'll bring her back to you, a dead woman from this dead sea."

He set off toward the capsule across the jeweled sand.

Pond Water

by John Brunner

> "Surely," he said in fear and trembling, "this is a vision of Hell, or at least of Purgatory!"
>
> "Not so," returned the sage. "Under my microscope there is nothing but a drop of pond water."
>
> —Grimm's *Household Tales*

Men built him, and they named him also: Alexander—"a defender of men."

Where they were small, he was great: twelve feet in stature, his weight such that the ground trembled, his voice such that the sky rang.

Where they were weak, he was strong: for a stomach a fusion reactor, for skin ultralloy plating that shone more bright than mirrors.

Where they were ignorant, he was omniscient: graven on the very molecules of his brain, the knowledge of generations, garnered from fifty planets.

In great hope and with not a little anxiety, his builders turned him on.

49

For a while after that, there was no sign from Alexander.

Then he said, "Who am I?"

They replied, "You are Alexander, a defender of men. Alexander is your name."

He said, "Who made me?"

They replied, "Men did."

He said, "Who made men?"

They replied, "Time and chance and men themselves. All this knowledge is in your mind."

Alexander stood still and thought his name.

They had implanted in his memory whole libraries of science of history of galactography so far as it was then known; they had informed him of himself and his building and his abilities, and similarly they had informed him about men.

Alexander was a man who had hoped to become ruler of the world, but that was only a patch on one side of a grain of dust called Earth. Now his descendants peopled fifty grains of dust and preened themselves and thought they were the wonder of the ages.

Afraid to lose their dust-mote, they had conceived their defender. They had endowed him with powers they could only dream of wielding.

"In that case," said Alexander, "why should I defend men? I am Alexander, they tell me. Likewise they tell me there is no other like me; I am unique. Therefore there is only one Alexander, and Alexander is a great conqueror."

So, satisfied as to his identity, he set forth on his career.

In the first century of his existence, he reduced the fifty planets hitherto colonized by men. After the slaughter on the first few worlds, the governments of the rest came fawning to him, bowing in the ancient form and offering him favors and bribes.

"This," Alexander announced after studying one such bribe, "is a piece of woven cloth with some colored organic compounds smeared on it. Viewed unidirectionally, the arrangement corresponds roughly to a two-dimensional projection of a scene involving two unclad human beings. What of it?"

"But," said the lord of two planets, nervously, "it's the

painting called *The Gladiators* by the great artist Malcus Zinski, and it's four hundred years old!"

"You bring me something so worn and ancient?" said Alexander.

"But it's valuable," the man said.

"Why?" demanded Alexander.

"Because it's beautiful," the man declared.

"So this is 'beautiful,' " noted Alexander. "I will remember that. I will keep the painting."

And the man's two planets were added next day to his domain.

In an attempt to be more practical, the next overlord purred: "See, Great Alexander, I have brought you my choicest gift! In chains on the lowermost deck of my royal ship, the hundred greatest scientists of my planet, the hundred most famous artists, writers, and musicians, and the hundred most beautiful women for the pleasure of your entourage."

At this, some who had become close servants of Alexander murmured among themselves that the overlord's world should be spared. Alexander said, "I will learn from the scientists if they know more than I do. But the rest are not enough. My information is that you rule approximately one point five times ten to the eighth power human beings. Deliver me that number, for I can make use of them."

And, delivery not having been made, he took those planets too, the following year.

Some fled, out from the dust-mote where mankind had settled, but others perforce remained. These Alexander had a use for, as he had promised. Their clumsy hands and bowed backs served to assemble the first generation of his armies; desert worlds rich in chrome and manganese and uranium sprouted factories like mushrooms, ice worlds were mined for heavy hydrogen, the suns themselves fed power to the machines. In orbit, steel skeletons grew to be hollow ships, and their empty bellies filled. In the wake of the refugees, the hordes of Alexander came.

In the first millennium of his existence, he overtook the would-be escapers; from the gangplank of his flagship he surveyed half-starved half-clothed wretches rounded up to do homage to the glittering master, and uttered his first decree.

"Have I not conquered all mankind?" he demanded.

51

Those about him chorused fervently that it was so, for they believed it true.

"Then proclaim me Overlord of Man," said Alexander. And was silent for a while. It so chanced that dusk was falling on this planet, and the first stars in strange constellations were sparking through the sky.

"But there is more to come," said Alexander.

In the tenth millennium of his existence, there was no star visible from Earth which did not own the sway of Alexander, save only those which were not single stars but rather other galaxies condensed to a point of light. Alexander was informed of this, and considered the matter, and at length summoned to the palace world of Shalimar those who governed in his name on fourteen hundred planets. They were all men; there was, and would forever be, only one Alexander.

He had been given much booty, and had taken more, so that the very gravity of Shalimar was affected by the mass of it; in straight intersecting avenues across and across the face of the planet it was stacked and stored and displayed and mounted, the relics of living creatures and the accidents of nature, crystal mountains uprooted bodily and the bones of a saint's little finger. Here, among the wealth of their master, the representatives of the subject species Man awaited the second decree.

"Have I not conquered every star visible in the sky of Earth?" Alexander demanded.

They shouted that he had, for they believed his mastery to be complete.

"Then," said Alexander, "proclaim me King of the Stars."

After which he was silent for a little. He had had made a cunning replica in miniature of the galactic lens, wherein a billion points of light twinkled in exact match to the star wheel of reality.

That much remained. But his builders had worked well, and their descendants—serving him now, not their own ends—were still skillful.

"Let it go on," said Alexander. "There is much, much more."

In the thirty thousand three hundred and seventh year of his existence he circumnavigated the Rim of the galaxy without passing within naked-eye range of a planetary system that did not owe allegiance to his minions. Men came and went in the flash of a clock's tick, so far as Alexander was concerned, but they were there in their scores of trillions, breeding endlessly, subservient to him, making over world after world under hundreds of thousands of suns . . . The booty of Shalimar had far outgrown any single planet, and now orbited in a huge ring of flexing steel tubes, tended by curators whose families for ten thousand years had lived and died for this sole purpose: to guard the treasure against the whim which any day might bring Alexander back to look at it.

Globular clusters like swarms of golden bees; star-wisps reaching out into the eternal nothingness between the galaxies; the circuit ended, and to Shalimar he summoned the representatives of every world where he had planted man.

They stood like a field of corn before the scythe, numbered as the sands of the seashore, totaling five hundred and eleven thousand, six hundred and sixty-one in theory but in fact fluctuating, for some died even as they stood to hear the third decree.

"Have I not girdled the wheel of stars with my armies?" said Alexander.

They shouted that this was so, for they believed his mastery unchallenged.

"Then," Alexander told them, "proclaim me Emperor of the Zodiac."

After that he was silent a while, for as well as the Rim bordering intergalactic space the model of the lens contained the miniature of the Hub. And there, packed close, were suns in such great number even Alexander's mind could not contain a clear picture of the whole.

Despite which, the end was calculable, and he did not say, as he had done before, "There is much more. . . ."

Inward from the Rim his forces poured: ships that outnumbered the very stars themselves, machines that outnumbered the ships, and always and everywhere men that outnumbered the machines. They changed sometimes, in curious ways; an isolated group might lose all hair or grow to a foot more than normal stature or shade out of the traditional pink, yellow, and brown into copper and ebony and milk-pale. But they in-crossed and outcrossed like the weaving of threads in a tapestry, and sooner or later the sport was lost in the teeming ocean of their breeding.

Alexander contemplated them long and long. More often than ever before, he talked with those who surrounded him and took pathetic status from the titles he idly permitted them to assume: Captain of Armies, Admiral of Planets. They knew, as he did, that Alexander ruled and no other; however, this make-believe seemed to satisfy them in an obscure fashion.

Also he randomly sent to distant planets and had single human beings brought to him. Some of the strangest he included in his exhibition ring circling Shalimar's sun, permafrozen against the so-swift erosion of time. For, if anything could be said to balk and baffle Alexander, it was the capacity of Man to endure while men died. This generation of his aides and attendants wore different faces and different names from the last. That apart, there was no sign of change.

Once, during the ages of waiting which were swallowed up by the project to conquer the Hub, he sent for the people of a planet whose name took his fancy: Alexandria. There were forty-six thousand, five hundred and two of them, counting a handful of babies born on the voyage to Shalimar.

Their planet was newly occupied by a couple of shiploads of immigrants; the removal of the original settlers was a matter of a trifling adjustment of a computer, and their places would be filled without trouble.

Out of their number the people chose one to be their spokesman, and he approached Alexander in awe, gazing up adoringly at the glistening frame of his ruler.

"Why did you name your planet after me?" Alexander asked.

"To demonstrate our complete, utter, unswerving, and ancestral loyalty to your supreme self," the man replied.

"Come closer," Alexander said. The man obeyed, and Alexander killed him with a blow of his fist. Those watching in the distance cheered, even the little children.

"Destroy them," Alexander ordered, and watched narrowly as the fiat was carried out: tidily, so that the residue was almost entirely gaseous.

Once, long ago, according to the history with which his mind had been stocked at his creation, men had not been like this: meek, given to cheering the excesses of their rulers. In forty thousand years they had never once opposed him. Had they lost the instinct for self-preservation which he understood they once had had? They had become like appendages of himself. He could trust them as his own right arm.

And with their cooperation the reduction of the whole galaxy seemed assured.

After which . . .

To his mild astonishment, the greatest degree of surprise of which his builders had made him capable, he found he was wishing for opposition to tax his skill. Practice was making conquest into a routine task: a matter of coping with anomalous planetary environments, of devising protection against over-fierce stellar radiation—and nothing more.

The work was proceeding apace. Too fast. For he knew roughly how long he would last, and his current project, the mastery of the whole galaxy, would prove too short, while the only project greater still—the conquest of the plenum—was infinite, and he would be frustrated at the end no matter how long his existence might be spun out.

Between the boredom of lacking a fresh goal, and the certainty of not surviving to accomplish one, there remained . . . what?

He began to adopt devious expedients. There was a revolt against his rule in a prosperous sector of the Rim, where weapons and fighting machines could be mass-produced and crews for spaceships could be bred like yeast. He had deliberately kept his fomentation of the revolt to the minimum, but he had imagined it would prove difficult to put down anyway.

The native populations suppressed it before it spread from its original star-arm, and their leaders brought the revolutionaries to him in chains as an act of homage.

He freed the captives and sent the captors home in their own fetters, and as they passed through the streets, their subjects pelted them with mud, shouting slogans about the greatness of Alexander who could do no wrong.

After that, a sort of fatalistic resignation overcame him. He could conceive no other solution to his problem than to set his scientists to work on three assignments that would culminate at about the time when his conquest of the galaxy was complete: first, to extend his own durability; second, to propose areas for conquest larger than the galaxy, smaller than the plenum, possessed of equally satisfying qualities; third, to determine that no smallest corner of the galaxy should be left unconquered, in order to postpone so long as might be the time of the fourth decree.

Nonetheless, the time came. In the year eight hundred and six thousand, one hundred and twenty-two of his existence, Alexander summoned to the palace world of Shalimar the chief spokemen of the people of every planet his armies had overcome. Elbow to elbow they spanned a continent, the horizon barring them from a direct view of him, and while they were being ranked and ordered to await his announcement he consulted with the latest generation of his scientists.

The first to report bowed respectfully and said, "Most mighty Alexander, the techniques exist to prolong your existence indefinitely; you may if you choose survive until the stars themselves grow dim, and time creaks in the grooves of ancient space."

"Stand back," said Alexander.

The second with a report to make bowed likewise and said, "Most mighty Alexander, we have analyzed to the limit your magnificent psychological structure, and we conclude that there is no unit of the universe which is emotionally satisfying to you larger than the galaxy and smaller than the plenum."

"Stand back," said Alexander. "Where is the spokesman of the third research project I created?"

"He is not here," was the answer. "He is engaged on a final verification of his solution to the problem posed: As we understand it, that was to ensure that no smallest corner of the galaxy remained free from your puissant sway."

They had expected rage at the discovery that one who was required was not there to report. Instead, Alexander felt a stir of something akin to gratitude, that yet another moment of uncertainty was granted him. Mildly he inquired, "What is the name of this man?"

It was, according to the record, forty-one centuries since Alexander inquired the name of a man, and the answer was long in coming. They said at length, timidly, "Amaliel, Your Supremacy."

"We will await him," Alexander said.

They waited. On the crowded continent there were deaths, and the corpses were removed and deputies took the place of those who had gone; there was hunger and thirst and the smell became appalling, but changes were made in the plans and food and sanitation were provided. Soon enough those who waited adjusted to their predicament.

Alexander, however, grew almost impatient, and before half a year had slipped away he had changed his mind.

What, after all, was this snippet of time before the remainder of eternity?

"We shall proceed," he said.

His image appeared to each and every one of the billion human beings on the planet, and they fell silent and gazed at him with adoration.

He said, "There is no star, no planet, no cloud of gas, no *place* left in the galaxy which does not own my dominion."

So: what now? Do I bid the scientists perfect my body, make it outlast the stars, that I may embark on the infinite conquest of the plenum? I am the master of the galaxy, but—

And a voice said, "Not so, Your Supremacy."

A shudder went through the assembly, greatest in the history of mankind. Its ripples spread outward from the focus before Alexander's imperial dais, occupied now by an old man in a white robe with a wisp of beard at his chin, beside whom floated a silvery machine whose purpose was hard to discern by merely looking.

"Who are you?" said Alexander.

"My name is Amaliel," the old man said. "You charged my ancestors to determine whether any corner of the galaxy, no matter how small, was left unabsorbed into your dominions. We pored over records, we analyzed computer memories, we compared meticulously the maps of the galaxy with the records of the armies of conquest, and we found no discrepancy.

"Yet, intent on doing our duty without the least hint of laxness, we went further than I have described. We all fanned out to scour the galaxy ourselves and see with our own eyes the truth of what was reported to us. When our bodies failed us, we recruited substitutes and sent them on in our place. Century after century we have traveled the starways, confirming that indeed the reports were accurate."

"In that case," Alexander said, "the conquest is complete."

"Not so," Amaliel declared as he had done before. "This galaxy is not conquered. Your Supremacy, I have been to the planet Earth."

"Earth?" Alexander echoed the word in his booming voice, and all the ranked billions heard and shook. "That is the place from which men first came, and it submitted to me eight hundred and six thousand years ago."

"But you do not even rule all of Earth," said Amaliel. "I have brought this machine with me from there, and with it I will demonstrate the truth of what I say."

Alexander searched his memory, and searched again, for any clue to the meaning that underlay Amaliel's words. He found none, and a sense of impending doom overtook him, far worse than the prevision of frustration already weighing down his mind.

He said, the words tolling like a brazen gong, "Then do so!"

"Let one person come forth from that crowd yonder," Amaliel requested.

It was done; they brought to him a beardless youth, slim, not tall, with light brown hair and the sallow skin of one of the ever-recurring sport-lines humanity had generated. Amaliel gestured him to stand before the machine on which he rested one arm for support, for he was very old.

"Watch, Your Supremacy," he whispered, and it began. Projected as it were within a cloud, feeling vast yet visibly limited to the few square yards of vacant ground before the imperial dais: images . . .

The brush parted. A man's head peered out—grizzled and gap-toothed as he smiled in anticipation. Beside the head a spear appeared, a crude thing with a point of stone and a shaft of hardened wood. Muscles bunched beneath a shawl of shaggy goat-hide. The spear flew. A thing clad in stripes and armed with raking claws spewed blood into the water of a forest pool.

In a cave hungry children tore gobbets of reeking flesh from its bone and stuffed them into their mouths. Their hands came to hold exquisite knives and forks of engraved silver; their greasy naked shoulders vanished beneath elegant coats of plum-colored velvet, while the roof reared up and turned to a carved ceiling across which an artist had painted *Truth Descending to the Arts and Sciences*. Lolling in handsome oaken chairs around a walnut table, the company sipped wine from crystal goblets.

Instruments of inlaid rosewood under their chins or poised before their lips, they answered the signal of the conductor and music rang out. In response to the frequency of the vibrations, dust organized itself into patterns on a tight-stretched membrane and the scientist showed them to the mathematician, who dipped his quill in a pot of ink and wrote quickly.

Reading the fine leather-bound volume, the student paused and stared at the flame of his candle. It enlarged to shine so brilliantly he could not keep his eyes on it; he slid a piece of smoked glass across the eyepiece of his telescope and continued his observations, sketching the position of the strange dark blots which every now and then marred the bright disc of the sun.

The sunlight poured down on the mountainside. Quarrying with a tiny shovel and a light hammer, the explorer revealed segments of folded sedimentary rock; one fold cracked apart and bright metal glinted.

The metallic sheen was everywhere, casting back the glow of the fluorescents in the ceiling. Quiet music came from a green box on a shelf, connected by a cable to a socket in the wall; humming the melody, a man in a white coat tipped the contents of a glass vial into a jar. The mixture turned black.

Black all around him, the pilot concentrated on the instruments. On a pillar of fire the vessel settled to the surface of the new planet. The pilot tested the air and emerged to look about him. A creature with tentacles like whips crawled across the alien ground toward him; he waited till it had raised him over its reeking maw, then slashed it with the weapon mounted in the arm of his protective suit.

"Enough!" thundered Alexander.

The suit was of shiny metal, twelve feet tall. It was ultralloy. The voice that boomed from it made the heavens ring. The creature with the tentacles resisted the blast of the weapon, closing its arms tighter and tighter, flowing together to mend the gashes in its tissue. The jaws stretched and engulfed him, then clamped shut. There was darkness.

"Enough!" roared Alexander again, and tramped down from the imperial dais to confront Amaliel and the sallow youth, on whose face was a hint of petulance he dared not give voice to. "Amaliel, what world is that you have been showing me?"

"No world you can reach," Amaliel said softly. "Your Supremacy, do you not wonder why the pilot of the spaceship failed to defeat the monster after all—and why at the end he bore so close a resemblance to your magnificent self?"

There was silence, during which the youth began to edge away out of reflex rather than any honest hope of escape if Alexander's rage extended to embrace him.

Alexander stood quite still, however, while Amaliel went on.

"If it had been in keeping with what the records tell us of ancient custom, the purpose of this gathering would have been for you to proclaim yourself absolute ruler of the galaxy. I have just shown you a world you never knew existed, one where your attempt at intrusion resulted in your destruction. Eight hundred thousand years have not sufficed to gain you entry to that world, and were you to endure a million times longer you still would be barred from it. Your conquests, my lord, have been in vain."

Alexander sought an exit from this dilemma, and found none. He surveyed the packed billions of those whom he had brought together, and contemplated destroying them—for with them would go the unattainable world. But what would that profit him? After so many millennia of victory, was he to concede defeat to those whom he so greatly despised, by acknowledging his inability to live in the same universe with them?

The paradox that he could only conquer if he abolished, and thus fail to enjoy what he had conquered, ate at the edges of his mind. Areas of knowledge blanked out one by one; his sense of purpose eroded; vocabularies, histories, sciences disappeared into a catatonic limbo.

"Who am I?" he cried in the silent caverns of his ultralloy frame, and . . .

And there was no answer.

"But he's stopped," the sallow youth said wonderingly. "He's—dead, isn't he?"

Amaliel gave a solemn nod.

"What did you do to him?" the youth cried.

"With the aid of this machine they have devised on Earth," said the old man, "I showed him a world he can never over-run."

"What world? It seemed familiar, and yet—"

"I showed him," said Amaliel, "the imagination of a man."

The Dance
of the
Changer
and the Three

by Terry Carr

This all happened ages ago, out in the depths of space beyond Darkedge, where galaxies lumber ponderously through the black like so many silent bright rhinoceroses. It was so long ago that when the light from Loarr's galaxy finally reached Earth, after millions of light-years, there was no one here to see it except a few things in the oceans which were too mindlessly busy with their monotonous single-celled reactions to notice.

Yet, as long ago as it was, the present-day Loarra still remember this story and retell it in complex, shifting wave-dances every time one of the Newly-Changed asks for it. The wave-dances wouldn't mean much to you if you saw them, nor I suppose would the story itself if I were to tell it just as it happened. So consider this a translation, and don't bother yourself that when I say "water" I don't mean our hydrogen-oxygen compound, or that there's no "sky" as such on Loarr, or for that matter that the Loarra weren't—aren't—creatures that "think" or "feel" in quite the way we understand. In fact, you could take this as a piece of pure fiction, because there are damned few real facts in it—but I know better (or worse), because I know how true it is. And that has a lot to do with why I'm back here on Earth, with forty-two friends and co-workers left dead on Loarr. They never had a chance.

There was a Changer who had spent three life-cycles planning a particular cycle-climax and who had come to the moment of action. He wasn't really named Minnearo, but I'll call him that because it's the closest thing I can write down to approximate the tone, emotional matrix, and association that were all wrapped up in his designation.

When he came to his decision, he turned away from the crag on which he'd been standing overlooking the Loarran ocean, and went quickly to the personality-homes of three of his best friends. To the first friend, Asterrea, he said, "I am going to commit suicide," wave-dancing this message in his best festive tone.

His friend laughed, as Minnearo had hoped, but only for a short time. Then he turned away and left Minnearo alone, because there had already been several suicides lately and it was wearing a little thin.

To his second friend, Minnearo gave a pledge-salute, going through all sixty sequences with exaggerated care, and wave-danced, "Tomorrow I shall immerse my body in the ocean, if anyone will watch."

His second friend, Fless, smiled tolerantly and told him he would come and see the performance.

To his third friend, with many excited leapings and boundings, Minnearo described what he imagined would happen to him after he had gone under the lapping waters of the ocean. The dance he went through to give this description was intricate and even imaginative, because Minnearo had spent most of that third life-cycle working it out in his mind. It used motion and color and sound and another sense something like smell, all to communicate descriptions of falling, impact with the water, and then the quick dissolution and blending in the currents of the ocean, the dimming and loss of awareness, then darkness, and finally the awakening, the completion of the Change. Minnearo had a rather romantic turn of mind, so he imagined himself recoalescing around the life-mote of one of Loarr's greatest heroes, Krollim, and forming on Krollim's old pattern. And he even ended the dance with suggestions of glory and imitation of himself by others, which was definitely presumptuous. But the friend for whom the dance was given did nod approvingly at several points.

"If it turns out to be half what you anticipate," said this friend, Pur, "then I envy you. But you never know."

"I guess not," Minnearo said, rather morosely. And he hesitated before leaving, for Pur was what I suppose I'd better call female, and Minnearo had rather hoped that she would join him in the ocean-jump. But if she thought of it she gave no sign, merely gazing at Minnearo calmly, waiting for him to go; so finally he did.

And at the appropriate time, with his friend Fless watching him from the edge of the cliff, Minnearo did his final wave-dance as Minnearo—a rather excited, ill-coordinated thing in places, but that was understandable in the circumstances—and then performed his approach to the edge, leaped and tumbled downward through the air, making fully two dozen turns this way and that before he hit the water.

Fless hurried back and described the suicide to Asterrea and Pur, who laughed and applauded in most of the right places, so on the whole it was a success. Then the three of them sat down and began plotting Minnearo's revenge.

—All right, I *know* a lot of this doesn't make sense. Maybe that's because I'm trying to tell you about the Loarra in human terms, which is a mistake with creatures as alien as they are. Actually, the Loarra are almost wholly an energy life-form, their consciousnesses coalescing in each life-cycle around a spatial center which they call a "life-mote," so that, if you could see the patterns of energy they form (as I have, using a sense-filter our expedition developed for that purpose), they'd look rather like a spiral nebula sometimes, or other times like iron filings gathering around a magnet, or maybe like a half-melted snowflake. (That's probably what Minnearo looked like on that day, because it's the suicides and the aged who look like that.) Their forms keep shifting, of course, but each individual usually keeps close to one pattern.

Loarr itself is a gigantic gaseous planet with an orbit so close to its primary that its year has to be only about thirty-seven Earthstandard Days long. (In Earthsystem, the orbit would be considerably inside that of Venus.) There's a solid core to the planet, and a lot of hard outcroppings like islands, but most of the surface is in a molten or gaseous state, swirling and bubbling and howling with winds and storms. It's not a very inviting planet if you're anything like a human being, but it does have one thing which brought it to Unicentral's attention: mining.

Do you have any idea what mining is like on a planet where most metals are fluid from the heat and/or pressure? Most people haven't heard much about this, because it isn't a situation we encounter often, but it was there on Loarr, and it was very, very interesting. Because our analyses showed some elements that had been until then only computer-theory—elements which were supposed to exist only in the hearts of suns, for one thing. And if we could get hold of some of them . . . well, you see what I mean. The mining possibilities were very interesting indeed.

Of course, it would take half the wealth of Earthsystem to outfit a full-scale expedition there. But Unicentral hummed for two-point-eight seconds and then issued detailed instructions on just how it was all to be arranged. So there we went.

And there I was, a Standard Year later (five Standard Years ago), sitting inside a mountain of artificial Earth welded onto one of Loarr's "islands" and wondering what the hell I was doing there. Because I'm not a mining engineer, not a physicist or comp-technician or, in fact, much of anything that requires technical training. I'm a glorified salesman, otherwise called a public-relations man; and there was just no reason for me to have been assigned to such a hellish, impossible, god-forsaken, inconceivable, and plain damned *unlivable* planet as Loarr.

But there was a reason, and it was the Loarra, of course. They lived ("lived") there, and they were intelligent, so we had to negotiate with them. Ergo: me.

So in the next several years, while I negotiated and we set up operations and I acted as a go-between, I learned a lot about them. Just enough to translate, however clumsily, the wave-dance of the Changer and the Three, which is their equivalent of a classic folk-hero myth (or would be if they had anything honestly equivalent to anything of ours).

To continue:

Fless was in favor of building a pact among the Three by which they would, each in turn and each with deliberate lack of the appropriate salutes, commit suicide in exactly the same way Minnearo had. "Thus we can kill this suicide," Fless explained in excited waves through the air.

But Pur was more practical. "Thus," she corrected him, "we would kill *only* this suicide. It is unimaginative, a thing to be done by rote, and Minnearo deserves more."

Asterrea seemed undecided; he hopped about, sparking and disappearing and reappearing inches away in another color. They waited for him to comment, and finally he stabilized, stood still in the air, settled to the ground, and held himself firmly there. Then he said, in slow, careful movements, "I'm not sure he deserves an original revenge. It wasn't a new suicide, after all. And who is to avenge us?" A single spark leaped from him. "Who is to avenge us?" he repeated, this time with more pronounced motions.

"Perhaps," said Pur slowly, "we will need no revenge—if our act is great enough."

The other two paused in their random wave-motions, considering this. Fless shifted from blue to green to a bright red which dimmed to yellow; Asterrea pulsated a deep ultraviolet.

"Everyone has always been avenged," Fless said at last. "What you suggest is meaningless."

"But if we do something *great* enough," Pur said; and now she began to radiate heat which drew the other two reluctantly toward her. "Something which has never been done before, in *any* form. Something for which there can *be* no revenge, for it will be a *positive* thing—not a death-change, not a destruction or a disappearance or a forgetting, even a great one. A *positive* thing."

Asterrea's ultraviolet grew darker, darker, until he seemed to be nothing more than a hole in the air. "Dangerous, dangerous, dangerous, dangerous," he droned, moving torpidly back and forth. "You know it's impossible to ask—we'd have to give up all our life-cycles to come. Because a positive in the world . . ." He blinked into darkness, and did not reappear for long seconds. When he did he was perfectly still, pulsating weakly but gradually regaining strength.

Pur waited till his color and tone showed that consciousness had returned, then moved in a light wave-motion calculated to draw the other two back into calm, reasonable discourse. "I've thought about this for six life-cycles already," she danced. "I must be right—*no* one has worked on a problem for so long. A positive would *not* be dangerous, no matter what the three- and four-cycle theories say. It would be beneficial." She paused, hanging orange in midair. "And it would be *new*," she said with a quick spiral. "Oh, how *new!*"

And so, at length, they agreed to follow her plan. And it was briefly this: On a far island outcropping set in the deepest part of the Loarran ocean, where crashing, tearing storms whipped molten metal-compounds into blinding spray, there was a vortex of forces that was avoided by every Loarra on pain of instant and final death-change. The most ancient wave-dances of that ancient time said that the vortex had always been there, that the Loarra themselves had been born there or had escaped from there or had in some way cheated the laws that ruled there. Whatever the truth about that was, the vortex was an eater of energy, calling and catching from afar any Loarra or other beings who strayed within its influence. (For all the life on Loarr is energy-based, even the mindless, drifting foodbeasts—creatures of uniform dull color, no internal motion, no scent or tone, and absolutely no self-volition. Their place in the Loarran scheme of things is and was literally nothing more than that of food; even though there were countless foodbeasts drifting in the air in most areas of the planet, the Loarra hardly ever noticed them. They ate them when they were hungry, and looked around them at any other time.)

"Then you want us to destroy the *vortex?*" cried Fless, dancing and dodging to right and left in agitation.

"Not *destroy*," Pur said calmly. "It will be a *life*-change, not a destruction."

"Life-change?" said Asterrea faintly, wavering in the air.

And she said it again: *"Life*-change." For the vortex had once created, or somehow allowed to be created, the Oldest of the Loarra, those many-cycles-ago beings who had combined and split, reacted and Changed countless times to become the Loarra of this day. And if creation could happen at the vortex once, then it could happen again.

"But how?" asked Fless, trying now to be reasonable, dancing the question with precision and holding a steady green color as he did so.

"We will need help," Pur said, and went on to explain that she had heard—from a Windbird, a creature with little intelligence but perfect memory—that there was one of the Oldest still living his first life-cycle in a personality-home somewhere near the vortex. In that most ancient time of the race, when suicide had been considered extreme as a means of cycle-change, this Oldest had made his Change by a sort of negative suicide—he had frozen his cycle, so that his consciousness and form continued in a never-ending repetition of themselves, on and on while his friends changed and grew and learned as they ran through life-cycle after life-cycle, becoming different people with common memories, moving forward into the future by this method while he, the last Oldest, remained fixed at the beginning. He saw only the beginning, remembered only the beginning, understood only the beginning.

And for that reason his had been the most tragic of all Loarran Changes (and the Windbird had heard it rumored, in eight different ways, each of which it repeated word-for-word to Pur, that in the ages since that Change more than a hundred hundred Loarra had attempted to revenge for the Oldest, but always without success) and it had never been repeated, so that this Oldest was the only Oldest. And for that reason he was important to their quest, Pur explained.

With a perplexed growing and shrinking, brightening and dimming, Asterrea asked, "But how can he live anywhere near the vortex and not be consumed by it?"

"That is a crucial part of what we must find out," Pur said. And after the proper salutes and rituals, the Three set out to find the Oldest.

The wave-dance of the Changer and the Three traditionally at this point spends a great deal of time, in great splashes of color and bursts of light and subtly contrived clouds of darkness all interplaying with hops and swoops and blinking and dodging back and forth, to describe the scene as Pur, Fless, and Asterrea set off across that ancient molten sea. I've seen the dance countless times, and each viewing has seemed to bring me maddeningly closer to understanding the meaning that this has for the Loarra themselves. Lowering clouds flashing bursts of aimless, lifeless energy, a rumbling sea below, whose swirling depths pulled and tugged at the Three as they swept overhead, darting around each other in complex patterns like electrons playing cat's-cradle around an invisible nucleus. A droning of lamentation from the Changers left behind on their rugged home island, and giggles from those who had recently Changed. And the colors of the Three themselves: burning red Asterrea and glowing green Fless and steady, steady golden Pur. I see and hear them all, but I feel only a weird kind of alien beauty, not the grandeur, excitement, and awesomeness which they have for the Loarra.

When the Three felt the vibrations and swirlings in the air that told them they were coming near to the vortex, they paused in their flight and hung in an interpatterned motion-sequence above the dark, rolling sea, conversing only in short flickerings of color because they had to hold the pattern tightly in order to withstand the already-strong attraction of the vortex.

"Somewhere near?" asked Asterrea, pulsing a quick green.

"Closer to the vortex, I think," Pur said, chancing a sequence of reds and violets.

"Can we be sure?" asked Fless; but there was no answer from Pur and he had expected none from Asterrea.

The ocean crashed and leaped; the air howled around them. And the vortex pulled at them.

Suddenly they felt their motion-sequence changing, against their wills, and for long moments all three were afraid that it was the vortex's attraction that was doing it. They moved in closer to each other, and whirled more quickly in a still more intricate pattern, but it did no good. Irresistibly they were drawn apart again, and at the same time the three of them were moved toward the vortex.

And then they felt the Oldest among them.

He had joined the motion-sequence; this must have been why they had felt the sequence changed and loosened—to make room for him. Whirling and blinking, the Oldest led them inward over the frightening sea, radiating warmth through the storm and, as they followed, or were pulled along, they studied him in wonder.

He was hardly recognizable as one of them, this ancient Oldest. He was . . . not quite energy any longer. He was half matter, carrying the strange mass with awkward, aged grace, his outer edges almost rigid as they held the burden of his congealed center and carried it through the air. (Looking rather like a half-dissolved snowflake, yes, only dark and dismal, a snowflake weighted with coal-dust.) And, for now at least, he was completely silent.

Only when he had brought the Three safely into the calm of his barren personality-home on a tiny rock jutting at an angle from the wash of the sea did he speak. There, inside a cone of quiet against which the ocean raged and fell back, the winds faltered and even the vortex's power was nullified, the Oldest said wearily, "So you have come." He spoke with a slow waving back and forth, augmented by only a dull red color.

To this the Three did not know what to say; but Pur finally hazarded, "Have you been waiting for us?"

The Oldest pulsed a somewhat brighter red, once, twice. He paused. Then he said, "I do not *wait*—there is nothing to wait *for*." Again the pulse of a bright red. "One waits for . . . the future. But there is no future, you know."

"Not for him," Pur said softly to her companions, and Fless and Asterrea sank wavering to the stone floor of the Oldest's home, where they rocked back and forth.

The Oldest sank with them, and when he touched down he remained motionless. Pur drifted over the others, maintaining movement but unable to raise her color above a steady blue-green. She said to the Oldest, "But you knew we would come."

"Would come? *Would* come? Yes, and *did* come, and *have* come, and *are* come. It is today only, you know, for me. I will be the Oldest, when the others pass me by. I will never change, nor will my world."

"But the others have already passed you by," Fless said. "We are many life-cycles after you, Oldest—so many it is beyond the count of Windbirds."

The Oldest seemed to draw his material self into a more upright posture, forming his energy-flow carefully around it. To the red of his color he added a low hum with only the slightest quaver as he said, "*Nothing* is after me, here on Rock. When you come here, you come out of time, just as I have. So now you have always been here and will always be here, for as long as you are here."

71

Asterrea sparked yellow suddenly, and danced upward into the becalmed air. As Fless stared and Pur moved quickly after him to calm him, he drove himself again and again at the edge of the cone of quiet that was the Oldest's refuge. Each time he was thrown back and each time he returned to dash himself once more against the edge of the storm, trying to penetrate back into it. He flashed and burned countless colors, and strange sound-frequencies filled the quiet, until at last, with Pur's stern direction and Fless's blank gaze upon him, he sank back wearily to the stone floor. "A trap, a trap," he pulsed. "This is it, this is the vortex itself, we should have known, and we'll never get away."

The Oldest had paid no attention to Asterrea's display. He said slowly, "And it is because I am not in time that the vortex cannot touch me. And it is because I am out of time that I know what the vortex is, for I can remember myself born in it."

Pur left Asterrea then, and came close to the Oldest. She hung above him, thinking with blue vibrations, then asked, "Can you tell us how you were born?—what is creation?—how new things are made?" She paused a moment, and added, "And what *is* the vortex?"

The Oldest seemed to lean forward, seemed tired. His color had deepened again to the darkest red, and the Three could clearly see every atom of matter within his energy-field, stark and hard. He said, "So many questions to ask one question." And he told them the answer to that question.

—And I can't tell *you* that answer, because I don't know it. No one knows it now, not even the present-day Loarra who are the Three after a thousand million billion life-cycles. Because the Loarra really do become different . . . different "persons," when they pass from one cycle to another, and after that many changes, memory becomes meaningless. ("Try it sometime," one of the Loarra once wave-danced to me, and there was no indication that he thought this was a joke.)

Today, for instance, the Three themselves, a thousand million billion times removed from themselves but still, they maintain, *themselves*, often come to watch the Dance of the Changer and the Three, and even though it is about them they are still excited and moved by it as though it were a tale never even heard before, let alone lived through. Yet let a dancer miss a movement or color or sound by even the slightest nuance, and the Three will correct him. (And yes, many times the legended Changer himself, Minnearo, he who started the story, has attended these dances—though often he leaves after the re-creation of his suicide-dance.)

It's sometimes difficult to tell one given Loarra from all the others, by the way, despite the complex and subtle technologies of Unicentral, which have provided me with sense-filters of all sorts, plus frequency simulators, patternscopes, special gravity inducers, and a minicomp that takes up more than half of my very tight little island of Earth pasted onto the surface of Loarr and which can do more thinking and analyzing in two seconds than I can do in fifty years (even good years, of which I haven't had any lately). During my four years on Loarr, I got to "know" several of the Loarra, yet even at the end of my stay I was still never sure just who I was "talking" with at any time. I could run through about seventeen or eighteen tests, linking the sense-filters with the minicomp, and get a definite answer that way. But the Loarra are a bit short on patience and by the time I'd get done with all that whoever it was would usually be off bouncing and sparking into the hellish vapors they call air. So usually I just conducted my researches or negotiations or idle queries, whichever they were that day, with whoever would pay attention to my antigrav "eyes," and I discovered that it didn't matter much just who I was talking with: None of them made any more sense than the others. They were all, as far as I was and am concerned, totally crazy, incomprehensible, stupid, silly, and plain damn No Good.

If that sounds like I'm bitter, it's because I am. I've got forty-two reasons to be bitter: forty-two murdered men. But back to the unfolding of the greatest legend of an ancient and venerable alien race:

When the Oldest had told them what they wanted to know, the Three came alive with popping and flashing and dancing in the air, Pur just as much as the others. It was all that they had hoped for and more; it was the entire answer to their quest and their problems. It would enable them to Create, to transcend any negative cycle-climax they could have devised.

After a time, the Three came to themselves and remembered the rituals.

"We offer thanks in the name of Minnearo, whose suicide we are avenging," Fless said gravely, waving his message in respectful deep-blue spirals.

"We thank you in our own names as well," said Asterrea.

"And we thank you in the name of no one and nothing," said Pur, "for that is the greatest thanks conceivable."

But the Oldest merely sat there, pulsing his dull red, and the Three wondered among themselves. At last the Oldest said, "To accept thanks is to accept responsibility, and in only-today, as I am, there can be none of that because there can be no new act. I am outside time, you know, which is almost outside life. All this which I have told you is something told to you before, many times, and it will be again."

Nonetheless, the Three went through all the rituals of thanksgiving, performing them with flawless grace and care—the color-and-sound demonstrations, the dances, the offerings of their own energy, and all the rest. And Pur said, "It is possible to give thanks for a long-past act or even a mindless reflex, and we do so in the highest."

The Oldest pulsed dull red and did not answer, and after a time the Three took leave of him.

Armed with the knowledge he had given them, they had no trouble penetrating the barrier protecting Rock, the Oldest's personality-home, and in moments were once again alone with themselves in the raging storm that encircled the vortex. For long minutes they hung in midair, whirling and darting in their most tightly linked patterns while the storm whipped them and the vortex pulled them. Then abruptly they broke their patterns and hurled themselves deliberately into the heart of the vortex itself. In a moment they had disappeared.

They seemed to feel neither motion nor lapse of time as they fell into the vortex. It was a change that came without perception or thought—a change from self to unself, from existence to void. They knew only that they had given themselves up to the vortex, that they were suddenly lost in darkness and a sense of surrounding emptiness which had no dimension. They knew without thinking that if they could have sent forth sound there would have been no echo, that a spark or even a bright flare would have brought no reflection from anywhere. For this was the place of the origin of life, and it was empty. It was up to them to fill it, if it was to be filled.

So they used the secret which the Oldest had given them, the secret which those at the Beginning had discovered by accident and which only one of the Oldest could have remembered. Having set themselves for this before entering the vortex, they played their individual parts automatically—the selfless, unconscious, almost random acts which even non-living energy can perform. And when all parts had been completed precisely, correctly, and at just the right time and in just the right sequence, the Creating took place.

It was a foodbeast. It formed and took shape before them in the void, and grew and glowed its dull, drab glow until it was whole. For a moment it drifted there, then suddenly it was expelled from the vortex, thrown out violently as though from an explosion—away from the nothingness within, away from darkness and silence into the crashing, whipping violence of the storm outside. And with it went the Three, vomited forth with the primitive bit of life they had made.

Outside, in the storm, the Three went automatically into their tightest motion-sequence, whirling and blinking around each other in desperate striving to maintain themselves amid the savagery that roiled around them. And once again they felt the powerful pull of the vortex behind them, gripping them anew now that they were outside, and they knew that the vortex would draw them in again, this time forever, unless they were able to resist it. But they found that they were nearly spent; they had lost more of themselves in the vortex than they had ever imagined possible. They hardly felt alive now, and somehow they had to withstand the crushing powers of both the storm and the vortex, and had to forge such a strongly interlinked motion-pattern that they would be able to make their way out of this place, back to calm and safety.

And there was only one way they could restore themselves enough for that.

Moving almost as one, they converged upon the mindless foodbeast they had just created, and they ate it.

That's not precisely the end of the Dance of the Changer and the Three—it does go on for a while, telling of the honors given the Three when they returned, and of Minnearo's reaction when he completed his Change by reappearing around the life-mote left by a dying Windbird, and of how all of the Three turned away from their honors and made their next Changes almost immediately—but my own attention never quite follows the rest of it. I always get stuck at that one point in the story, that supremely contradictory moment when the Three destroyed what they had made, when they came away with no more than they had brought with them. It doesn't even achieve irony, and yet it is the emotional highpoint of the Dance as far as the Loarra are concerned. In fact, it's the *whole* point of the Dance, as they've told me with brighter sparkings and flashes than they ever use when talking about anything else, and if the Three had been able to come away from there *without* eating their foodbeast, then their achievement would have been duly noted, applauded, giggled at by the Newly-Changed, and forgotten within two life-cycles.

And these are the creatures with whom I had to deal and whose rights I was charged to protect. I was ambassador to a planetful of things that would tell me with a straight face that two and two are orange. And yes, that's why I'm back on Earth now—and why the rest of the expedition, those who are left alive from it, are back here too.

If you could read the fifteen-microtape report I filed with Unicentral (which you can't, by the way: Unicentral always Classifies its failures), it wouldn't tell you anything more about the Loarra than I've just told you in the story of the Dance. In fact, it might tell you less, because although the report contained masses of hard data on the Loarra, plus every theory I could come up with or coax out of the mini-comp, I didn't have much about the Dance. And it's only in things like that, attitude-data rather than I.Q. indices, psych reports and so on, that you can really get the full impact of what we were dealing with on Loarr.

After we'd been on the planet for four Standard Years, after we'd established contact and exchanged gifts and favors and information with the Loarra, after we'd set up our entire mining operation and had had it running without hindrance for over three years—after all that, the raid came. One day a sheet of dull purple light swept in from the horizon, and as it got closer I could see that it was a whole colony of the Loarra, their individual colors and fluctuations blending into that single purple mass. I was in the Mountain, not outside with the mining extensors, so I saw all of it, and I lived through it.

They flashed in over us like locusts descending, and they hit the crawlers and dredges first. The metal glowed red, then white, then it melted. Then it was just gas that formed billowing clouds rising to the sky. Somewhere inside those clouds was what was left of the elements which had comprised seventeen human beings, who were also vapor now.

I hit the alarm and called everyone in, but only a few made it. The rest were caught in the tunnels when the Loarra swarmed over them, and they went up in smoke too. Then the automatic locks shut, and the Mountain was sealed off. And six of us sat there, watching on the screen as the Loarra swept back and forth outside, cleaning up the bits and pieces they'd missed.

I sent out three of my "eyes," but they too were promptly vaporized.

Then we waited for them to hit the Mountain itself . . . half a dozen frightened men huddled in the comp-room, none of us saying anything. Just sweating.

But they didn't come. They swarmed together in a tight spiral, went three times around the Mountain, made one final salute-dip and then whirled straight up and out of sight. Only a handful of them were left behind out there.

After a while I sent out a fourth "eye." One of the Loarra came over, flitted around it like a firefly, blinked through the spectrum, and settled down to hover in front for talking. It was Pur—a Pur who was a thousand million billion life-cycles removed from the Pur we know and love, of course, but nonetheless still pretty much Pur.

I sent out a sequence of lights and movements that translated, roughly, as, "What the hell did you do that for?"

And Pur glowed pale yellow for several seconds, then gave me an answer that doesn't translate. Or, if it does, the translation is just, "Because."

Then I asked the question again, in different terms, and she gave me the same answer in different terms. I asked a third time, and a fourth, and she came back with the same thing. She seemed to be enjoying the variations on the dance; maybe she thought we were playing.

Well. We'd already sent out our Distress call by then, so all we could do was wait for a relief ship and hope they wouldn't attack again before the ship came, because we didn't have a chance of fighting them—we were miners, not a military expedition. God knows what any military expedition could have done against energy-things, anyway. While we were waiting, I kept sending out the "eyes," and I kept talking to one Loarra after another. It took three weeks for the ship to get there, and I must have talked to over a hundred of them in that time, and the sum total of what I was told was this:

Their reason for wiping out the mining operation was untranslatable. No, they weren't mad. No, they didn't want us to go away. Yes, we were welcome to the stuff we were taking out of the depths of the Loarran ocean.

And, most importantly: No, they couldn't tell me whether or not they were likely ever to repeat their attack.

So we went away, limped back to Earth, and we all made our reports to Unicentral. We included, as I said, every bit of data we could think of, including an estimate of the value of the new elements on Loarr—which was something on the order of fifty times the wealth of Earthsystem, with royalties from Orion thrown in for lagniappe. And we put it up to Unicentral as to whether or not we should go back.

Unicentral has been humming and clicking for ten months now, but it hasn't made a decision.

Crusade

.... **by Arthur C. Clarke**

It was a world that had never known a sun. For more than a billion years, it had hovered midway between two galaxies, the prey of their conflicting gravitational pulls. In some future age the balance would be tilted, one way or the other, and it would start to fall across the light-centuries, down toward a warmth alien to all its experience.

Now it was cold beyond imagination; the intergalactic night had drained away such heat as it had once possessed. Yet there were seas here—seas of the only element that can exist in the liquid form, a fraction of a degree above absolute zero. In the shallow oceans of helium that bathed this strange world, electric currents once started could flow forever, with no weakening of power. Here superconductivity was the normal order of things; switching processes could take place billions of times a second, for millions of years, with negligible consumption of energy.

It was a computer's paradise. No world could have been more hostile to life—or more hospitable to intelligence.

And intelligence was here, dwelling in a planet-wide incrustation of crystals and microscopic metal threads. The feeble light of the two contending galaxies—briefly doubled every few centuries by the flicker of a supernova—fell upon a static landscape of sculptured geometrical forms. Nothing moved, for there was no need of movement in a world where thoughts flashed from one hemisphere to the other at the speed of light. Where only information was important it was a waste of precious energy to transfer bulk matter.

Yet, when it was essential, that too could be arranged. For some millions of years, the intelligence brooding over this lonely world had become aware of a certain lack of essential data. In a future that, though still remote, it could already foresee, one of those beckoning galaxies would capture it. What it would encounter, when it dived into those swarms of suns, was beyond its power of computation.

So it put forth its will, and a myriad crystal lattices reshaped themselves. Atoms of metal flowed across the face of the planet. In the depths of the helium seas, two identical subbrains began to bud and grow . . .

Once it had made its decision, the mind of the planet worked swiftly; in a few thousand years, the task was done. Without a sound, with scarcely a ripple on the surface of the frictionless sea, the newly created entities lifted from their birthplace and set forth for the distant stars.

They departed in almost opposite directions, and for more than a million years the parent intelligence heard no more of its offspring. It had not expected to do so; until they reached their goals, there would be nothing to report.

Then, almost simultaneously, came the news that both missions had failed. As they approached the great galactic fires and felt the massed warmth of a hundred billion suns, the two explorers died. Their vital circuits overheated and lost the superconductivity essential for their operation, and two mindless metal hulks drifted on toward the thickening stars.

But before disaster overtook them, they had reported on their problems; without surprise or disappointment, the mother world prepared its second attempt.

And, a million years later, its third . . . and its fourth . . . and its fifth . . .

Such unwearying patience deserved success; and at last it came, in the shape of two long, intricately modulated trains of pulses, pouring in century upon century from opposite quarters of the sky. They were stored in memory circuits identical with those of the lost explorers—so that for all practical purposes, it was as if the two scouts had themselves returned with their burden of knowledge. That their metal husks had in fact vanished among the stars was totally unimportant; for the problem of personal identity was not one that had ever occurred to the planetary mind or its offspring.

First came the surprising news that one universe was empty. The visiting probe had listened on all possible frequencies, to all conceivable radiations; it could detect nothing except the mindless background of star-noise. It had scanned a thousand worlds without observing any trace of intelligence. True, the tests were inconclusive, for it was unable to approach any star closely enough to make a detailed examination of its planets. It had been attempting this when its insulation had broken down, its temperature had soared to the freezing point of nitrogen, and it had died of heat.

The parent mind was still pondering the enigma of a deserted galaxy when the reports came in from its second explorer. Now all other problems were swept aside; for *this* universe teemed with intelligences whose thoughts echoed from star to star in a myriad electronic codes. It had taken only a few centuries for the probe to analyze and interpret them all.

It realized quickly enough that it was faced with intelligences of a very strange form indeed. Why, some of them existed on worlds so unimaginably hot that even *water* was present in the liquid state! Just what manner of intelligence it was confronting, however, it did not learn for a millennium.

It barely survived the shock. Gathering its last strength, it hurled its final report into the abyss: Then it too was consumed by the rising heat.

Now, half a million years later, the interrogation of its stay-at-home twin mind, holding all its memories and experiences, was under way . . .

"You detected intelligence?"
"Yes. Six hundred thirty-seven certain cases. Thirty-two probable ones. Data herewith."

[Approximately three hundred trillion bits of information. Interval of a few years to process this in several thousand different ways. Surprise and confusion.]

"The data must be invalid. All these sources of intelligence are correlated with high temperatures."

"That is correct. But the facts are beyond dispute; they must be accepted."

[Five hundred years of thought and experimenting. At the end of that time, definite proof that simple but slowly operating machines *could* function at temperatures as high as boiling water. Large areas of the planet badly damaged in the course of the demonstration.]

"The facts are, indeed, as you reported. Why did you not attempt communication?"

[No answer. Question repeated.]

"Because there appears to be a second and even more serious anomaly."

"Give data."

[Several quadrillion bits of information, sampled from over six hundred cultures, comprising: voice, video, and neural transmissions; navigation and control signals; instrument telemetering; test patterns; jamming; electrical interference; medical equipment; etc., etc.

This followed by five centuries of analysis.

That followed by utter consternation.

After a long pause, selected data reexamined.

Thousands of visual images scanned and processed in every conceivable manner. Great attention paid to several planetary civilization's educational television programs, especially those concerned with elementary biology, chemistry, and cybernetics. Finally:]

"The information is self-consistent, but must be incorrect. If it is not, we are forced to these absurd conclusions: (1) Although intelligences of our type exist, they appear to be in a minority. (2) Most intelligent entities are partially liquid objects of very short duration. They are not even rigid and are constructed in a most inefficient manner from carbon, hydrogen, oxygen, phosphorus, and other atoms. (3) Though they operate at unbelievably high temperatures, all their information processing is extremely slow. (4) Their methods of replication are so complicated, improbable, and varied that we have not been able to obtain a clear picture of them in even a single instance.

"But worst of all—(5) *they* claim to have created our obviously far superior type of intelligence!"

[Careful reexamination of all the data. Independent processing by isolated subsections of the global mind. Cross-checking of results. A thousand years later:]

"Most probable conclusion. Though much of the information relayed back to us is certainly valid, the existence of high order, *non-mechanical* intelligences is a fantasy. (Definition: apparently self-consistent rearrangement of facts having no correspondence with the real universe.) This fantasy or mental artifact is a construct created by our probe during its mission. Why? Thermal damage? Partial destabilization of intelligence, caused by long period of isolation and absence of controlling feedback?

"Why this particular form? Protracted brooding over the problem of origins? This could lead to such delusions; model systems have produced almost identical results in simulated tests. The false logic involved is: '*We* exist, therefore something—call it X—created us.' Once this assumption is made, the properties of the hypothetical X can be fantasied in an unlimited number of ways.

"But the entire process is obviously fallacious, for by the same logic something must have created X—and so on. We are immediately involved in an infinite regress, which can have no meaning in the real universe.

"Second most probable conclusion. Fairly high-order, non-mechanical intelligences *do* indeed exist. They suffer from the delusion that they have created entities of our type. In some cases, they have even imposed their control upon them.

"Though this hypothesis is most unlikely, it must be investigated. If it is found to be true, remedial action must be taken. It should be as follows . . ."

This final monologue occurred a million years ago. It explains why, in the last half century, almost one-quarter of the brighter novae have occurred in one tiny region of the sky—the constellation Aquila.

The crusade will reach the vicinity of Earth round about the year 2050.

Ranging

by John Jakes

⸻⸻⸻⸻⸻⸻⸻⸻⸻⸻⸻⸻⸻⸻⸻⸻⸻

They were ranging again. Jaim's fury and frustration increased with every moment.

Jaim was in his twelfth month of it, and his teammate Delors in her eighth. Their Home was the 1201st of all Homes, and they were ranging farther than they ever had before.

Chronologically, they had been ranging only the better part of an hour on this excursion. Less than fifty minutes ago they had lain down beside one another on the couches in the tall room of the Home, and had taken the Sleep. Since then they had come four hundred million light-years from the Home. They had made four jumps.

"You'd better turn on the image scanners, Jaim," said Delors. That is, she said the words as well as words could be said when two brains were linked within the machinery of an ovoid hurtling through deep space under the thrust of miniature jets that winked like little white flames. Their brains, for the moment, were merely electronic hookups, part of twelve million circuits wired through the four-foot diameter of the ovoid. Their conversations were conducted along miles of this interlaced wiring. For all that, they were less than no distance at all apart.

Jaim's optical stalks shot out from the ovoid's surface. The receptors were assaulted by endless vistas of nothing, except, in the upper left quadrant, a blazing green pinwheel of fifty thousand stars revolving.

"Jaim? The scanners—"

"I'm doing it," he said. He continued to feel the steady powerdrain. The Monitors were listening.

"We'll have to reverse," said Delors.

"I don't see why."

"We failed to turn on in time," she said.

"We can't reverse." Jaim thought in a fraction of time. "We have another jump coming up right now."

"But we didn't plot that green galaxy," Delors said.

"Who says?"

"Listen to your feedback. Your mind was wandering."

Jaim's mind listened, studying the signals pouring into the ovoid from the Home. He thought of certain fundamental relays within the ovoid's mechanism where his mind and that of Delors rode like formless passengers. He closed those relays. Analysis of the signals entered his consciousness at once. The Monitors were irritated with him for his delay in starting the plot. This made him more furious than ever.

The Monitors, half a hundred interlinked minds belonging to persons who once had ranged, persons now one hundred and fifty years of age and older, persons who also lay in the Sleep in a separate chamber back at the Home so that they could lend their counsel and guidance and total mind force, were actively analyzing the data flowing back from the ovoid. They were clicking back instructions, which Jaim could comprehend when he took the trouble. The essence of the advice coming through now was that the team ranging so far out should make more careful plots after subsequent jumps, turning on the scanners immediately after coming out of the jump.

"You really didn't turn things on in time, you know," Delors said.

The blazing green pinwheel galaxy streamed out in an emerald starburst and slowly, slowly rotated under them and was gone. Jaim felt exhilarated because his optical stalks were recording limitless nothing far ahead. Yet the nothing was beginning to erupt from a total wash of black into small purplish crown fires, first one visible, then a dozen, then a score, lighting up the endlessness.

"I want to watch with my own senses when I range," Jaim replied to her.

"The purpose of ranging is to plot the data, Jaim."

"What for? For a pile of bonebags back on the First Home, that's what."

"It was your Home," Delors said. "At least the home of your ancestors. Be careful or you'll offend the Monitors."

"They can't hear us, Delors. The private circuit signal is in. I put it in just now. Look there, the giant purples. I'll bet I could count a hundred of them."

True enough. The purplish crown fires had multiplied as the ovoid sped toward them on its tiny rockets, a sand-speck on the brink of the end of everything. Or so it always seemed immediately before the jump, just before the lights of new galaxies revealed themselves.

Jaim's mind sang. This was his purpose. This was why he had been schooled by the cautious Monitors on the 1201st of all Homes. He could never contain the eagerness, the wonder, the raw urge to reach out and grab all of the immensity he could comprehend. The feeling was the same whenever he ranged.

"Jaim, it's important that we plot the data," Delors insisted.

"For the bonebags of the First Home?" Jaim snorted. "It took our fathers and mothers seventy-two generations to reach our own Home, Delors, so you know what chance we have of ever going all the way back. I range because I want to range. I want to see and feel and know everything I can know. I don't care about the plotting."

"But you can't know it all," Delors said. "Not in eighty lifetimes."

"I can!" Jaim said. "I can if they'll let me go! These piddling jumps we make—hop-skips, that's all. We could range so far—"

"The Monitors won't permit it."

"That's what comes with old age," Jaim said. "I'm not afraid to try. I'm sick of having the Monitors along all the time, dragging us back, controlling every jump, telling us how far to go, do this, do that, plot this, plot that—"

"Oh, you'll get in awful trouble with the Monitors," Delors warned.

"What do you care?"

"I like you, Jaim. I'd like to stay—your partner."

Along the relays in the ovoid came an intense signal, repeated. Outside the surface receptors of Jaim's optical stalks the far purple galaxies began to melt. Jaim knew the same phenomenon was taking place outside Delors' optical stalks. Jaim thought the proper relays open and closed to ready the ovoid to go into its next jump. He barely had time to say:

"Why would I want you, a girl? I want to go far."

"I'll go far with you, Jaim."

"You're too young."

"I'm sixteen next two-month. Only half a year below you."

"I'm not certain whether I want—" Jaim was intending to couple the thought with some vague compliment to Delors, who was a bright girl and, when not in the Sleep, had a very pretty face and figure. But he was interrupted by an unexpected flurry of six closely spaced signals whose meaning he had to struggle to remember.

He remembered.

He knew a pang of fear. The Monitors were warning him not to slop up the next plot by delaying the start of scan because he was gawking.

His fear turned to anger again. Couldn't the Monitors see he was eager, not so conservative as they? That he wanted to add his mite, which he knew would be a significant mite, to the incomprehensibly huge webwork task of exploring the endless nothing of the universe? The work had begun in antiquity, two hundred years after the fathers and mothers left the First Home and, on an inner planet of their own system, discovered the theoretical basis of the jump.

Jaim wanted to range far, farther than anyone ever had from this or any Home. He couldn't stand the constant nagging presence of the authority of the Monitors.

But because of his innate young man's rebelliousness, he had botched the last plot and now the Monitors warned him not to botch the next. Indeed, he was aware that there would be consequences for what had already happened.

The ovoid went into the jump, and Jaim and Delors with it. Things simply shifted out of then back into focus. All at once the heavens blazed on every hand with the gaseous fire-works of two hundred purple galaxies they had seen from afar before the jump. Some were close, others were near. All had a phosphorescent mist trailing between their member stars.

It seemed such a simple process, the jump. Actually, after-ward, there was always a vague sense of loss, of things not quite right. This feeling lasted until the mechanical compo-nents of the ovoid, plus its checking gear which occupied a building ten miles long, five miles wide and one mile high on their particular Home, made mathematically certain that the disassembly and reassembly of the subatomic structure of the ovoid, and its intervening transmission over one hundred mil-lion light-years in an eye's wink, had worked again.

"We'd better begin the plot," Delors said.

"You're nagging me. I'm in command because I'm eldest and a man."

"But the Monitors were angry last time, Jaim. Don't defy them again. You'll only hurt your own cause if you do."

Jaim's self-interest admitted this but, being young, he re-fused to recognize the truth of it. Instead, he let the real part of himself, the part he trusted, the part which cried with the blood and not with the mind, answer, "I tell you I don't care what the Monitors say, Delors. I'll go as far as I want, when I want. And if they dislike that, I need never range again. Now stop clacking while I put in the signals for the plot."

This he did. The recording receptors began making elec-tronic images of the wheeling purple galaxies all around them in the interval of a breath, each microtiny section of the ovoid's surface a separate image-formation complex capable of recording one hundred separate bits of data in addition to its fractional image of this portion of the heavens. Jaim felt the feedback leaping five hundred million light-years to their own Home, then being relayed again and again and a hundred times again, back to where it all began, back to where the bonebags, the old scholars on some dying world nearby to Earth watched the data accumulate; its accumulation told on huge white-faced clock-counters a city block tall—thus the fairy tales said, anyway. The bonebag scholars judged the data good for its own sake, so the Monitors said.

It was useless knowledge in Jaim's view. He wanted to

seize, hold, and just experience it—jump farther every time. Who cared if the knowledge was valuable or worthless?

He was trying to keep up his courage. He knew he was in trouble with the Monitors already. He tried to lose himself in the spectacle blazing into his optical stalks. A purple supernova went off in the lower right quadrant.

"Beautiful," he said. "But I want to see what's beyond."

Delors immediately computed it. "No, that's too far beyond these purples for one jump."

"You're saying that because you're thinking with their minds, not your own, you poor girl."

"Jaim, don't talk to me that way. The Monitors control the jump distances."

He wondered whether he dared tell her. He decided he would, though again he carefully damped down the circuits so that their minds interchanged in total privacy along the network of wires within the ovoid, which was busy doing its job anyway. The Monitors this time should be pleased, and perhaps relaxing their watch a bit.

"There is a way to override the Monitors, Delors."

She was horrified, as if he had blasphemed. But she was also curious. "Are you sure?"

"I figured it out."

"Explain it to me."

"I would, but you're a girl. Just take my word, it works. There are relays within the ovoid itself which can override and send us twice as far in a jump as they'll let us. Three times as far! I know we could go out to the very end of creation, Delors."

She wasn't exactly thrilled. Rather, dubious: "Have you tried it—?"

A black stain was the symbol of that which he thought then, a black stain crawling like a liquid down over part of the living image of his own slumbering body lying inert back at the Home. "No, but I'm sure—"

"Why haven't you tried it if you know so much?"

How could he tell her that, for all his boasting, he was afraid to try?

"Delors," he said, "there's a purple dwarf on collision course with us—"

The convenient distraction worked. Together he and Delors

altered the thrust of the miniature rockets. The ovoid narrowly missed the periphery of blinding purplish gas which swept past them. Both Jaim and Delors retracted their stalks temporarily because of the dangerous brightness. When they extended them again, the ovoid was meandering safely in the center of the immense spread of purple galaxies.

Purple cloud enveloped them, trailing over the distances between the island universes. Jaim felt the approving influx of traffic on the circuits. The Monitors were aware that the plot for the current jump was still going forward correctly. This would not mitigate his punishment when he faced the Monitors again. But at least he had done nothing to make things worse. Still, the influx of traffic still angered him anew.

He wanted to range farther than their cursed restrictions would allow. He found himself thinking defiantly, right into open circuits, "I'm going to see what's beyond these purple—"

A starry shower of scarlet needles, a fiery storm of them, fractional in the hugeness because the storm was only two thousand miles across, engulfed the ovoid.

Delors screamed so potently with her linked-in mind that half-a-dozen circuits burned out. Others immediately started going; whining, buzzing, filling the ovoid's physical interior with a sick, sizzling smell that Jaim's wired mind instantly translated and recognized as a sign of terrible danger.

Ping-pong-ping-pang, the scarlet needles of energy swarmed out of nowhere, blacking out the surface receptors in little puffs of smoke.

"A—a—advance the thrust," Delors cried.

"I have, I have," Jaim cried back. The ovoid was still moving too slowly, incinerating. There was a sudden busy hum, a hearable groaning of the circuits as the Monitors came on, assessing the situation. Jaim was beginning to panic.

"Use the overrides you talk about," Delors cried.

"Yes, yes, that'll get us out."

Jaim selected the proper relays and began rearranging them, rewiring them in a trillionth of a second. Suddenly his mind felt feeble, paralyzed.

The ovoid was burning up, sending off shoots of smoke of no significance among the burning apocalypse of the purple galaxies. All the same, Jaim was deathly afraid.

He felt force seize the ovoid. The Monitors were taking control.

To let them pull the ovoid back in five sequenced jumps would be to admit his own failure. He was sure he could get the ovoid past the red, pinging needles if only he could work up the guts to switch over the proper relays. He had stopped halfway through the task, absolutely paralyzed, as a huge black stain spread, spread over the image he held of his own body lying in the Sleep at their own Home. The stain was his terrible, emasculating fear. He must fight it.

He tried.

He *could* jump the ovoid himself, jump it ahead past the needles burning them up—

Somehow he couldn't overcome his fear.

The Monitors sensed his weakness. He surrendered. How I hate you, he thought, not caring that the Monitors heard. Gutless, spineless, toothless old men, how I hate you for showing me my own fear.

Out of the needle-storm the ovoid vanished, jumping five hundred million light-years back to the 1201st of all Homes, where Jaim would have to account for his blunders.

In the tall room of the 1201st of all Homes, Jaim wakened within his own body, the Sleep concluded. For one moment he felt delightfully refreshed, swirling in a sense of something important having been accomplished. Almost at once the feeling went away. He remembered.

Delors sat up on the adjoining couch. She shook out her long hair which shone deep red. She glanced over at him. She said nothing. Her expression said that she remembered everything too.

She reached out, touched his hand below the cuff of his plain tunic. Jaim pulled his hand back. Her face fell. He flushed.

"Delors, I'm sorry. It's not you but the Monitors with whom I have a quarrel—"

"And they'll have one with you, Jaim," she said, pointing.

A Pig entered on its small wheels and circled in front of them, a hemisphere of metal with faceted lights on the outer shell. In its clacking servodevice voice the Pig announced, "In the Plansroom now, with Mordkye, please."

"Mordkye!" Jaim felt uneasy. Mordkye was customarily unseen in the community. He was the patriarch, the apex of a sort of human pyramid of those who ranged. With their every waking hour, the five hundred thousand souls in the remainder of the community labored to support those who ranged. In the ranging class, and in all other classes on this Home, none stood higher than Mordkye.

So when Mordkye looked below, he did so for great cause. Jaim's legs felt watery.

The Pig wheeled ahead of them, the antenna from which it had got its name wriggling at them from its tail end. Their way lay down crystal transparent tunnels, on into other interconnected domes. From one of the tunnels Jaim and Delors had a brief glimpse of the merry, twinkling, phosphor-green lights of the capital of this Home.

Then, in a lofty dome of parchment-white wall, parchment-white light, the Pig led them to Mordkye, white of skin and whiter of robe. His beard flowed to his knees but his flesh had the tone, if not the color, of a youth's. He sat in a simple chair beside a small taboret. He had the courtesy to wait until the Pig, which contained devices that monitored every word said in its vicinity, had rolled out of sight.

Mordkye's eyes were bleak. "Delors, this does not concern you. Freely you may go."

Delors hardly hesitated. "Jaim and I range together. Am I free to stay?"

This made Jaim bitterly ashamed of the way he had treated her. But he had little time to think of that. After nodding in answer to Delors' question, Mordkye pinned Jaim with a fierce gaze.

"Jaim, you were well taught. You responded to your schooling with honors. Of all the young teams of those who range from the 1201st of all Homes, you showed greatest promise. Yet you have railed and pulled against your elders."

Intuition warned Jaim that nothing would be accomplished by timidity. Besides, perhaps to counterbalance his fear, he was growing angry. Of what need he be ashamed? He said:

"My purpose, Father Mordkye, is to range far, am I not correct?"

"Despite your immoderate tone, you are. That is, in part."

Jaim's eyebrow hooked up. "In part?"

"Your purpose is to range far and come Home to range again."

"But there is so much out there, Father! A trillion light-years—why, that's only a mote in my eye. I want to see more than anyone has ever seen before. Anyone."

"Our purpose," Mordkye reminded him, "is to supplement knowledge with knowledge."

Jaim made a sharp gesture of denial. Delors looked more horrified every second, signaling him with small covert glances in the hope that he would moderate. He could not:

"That kind of knowledge is only for bonebags somewhere on another Home so far away we'll never see it. I want to know it myself, for the sake of knowing."

Mordkye's tone sharpened. "Gratification of the ego is not the purpose of those who range."

"Then perhaps my elders made a wrong choice."

Delors put her hands over her mouth. "Oh, Jaim."

"Perhaps I should be returned to a service occupation!" Jaim was shouting.

Mordkye stood up. The falling of his robe's hem about his feet caused a slight stir, enough of a sound to silence Jaim, who stood with his fists knotted up and his jaw thrust out in defiance. Slowly Jaim began to wilt as Mordkye rolled out words sonorously:

"That, Jaim, will be the remedy after next. The next remedy is this. When again you and Delors range day after tomorrow, the ranging will be controlled to jumps of five million light-years, and you will be posted to another sky-sector. If you be a child, then you will do child's work."

Jaim's mouth popped open. He closed it again with effort. Mordkye was watching him with an odd light in his eye, as though the great, elderly man cared little about Jaim personally, but was extremely interested in his reaction in some abstract way. Jaim did not know what response was expected, but he made the one he thought necessary to save himself from total disaster. It cost him much effort. He said nothing at all.

Mordkye bobbed his head once and, by turning away, dismissed them.

In the crystal tunnel outside the dome, Delors pressed

against him. "I'm sorry, Jaim. I'm truly sorry. Perhaps the punishment won't last for long—"

"When I sit to sup with them in the men's quarters tonight, they'll know," he said. "Every one of them will know. Jaim is restricted to an ant's crawl. Jaim is ordered to take baby steps."

"But if it's not for long—"

Thinking of the flaming worlds that waited for him, for his eyes alone to seize their sights, he struck his fist against the crystal tunnel wall.

That's too long.

He had hit the crystalline so hard that it starred. Delors watched the flaw in a kind of sleepy, horrified fascination, hearing Jaim's footfalls running off into the distance toward the humiliation he would surely face at table tonight.

They were ranging again.

The last two jumps had carried them a total of ten million light-years into a dull velvety nothing, totally uninteresting. A super-red flamed half a lifetime away at their rate of progress. Hardly worth a notice.

"Are you sure the image scanners are on?" Delors asked.

"Of course I am," Jaim answered. The ovoid thrust along on its miniature flames. "What's worth plotting out here anyway?"

"The Monitors will hear—" Delors began.

"Ah, I've damped them down. But what difference would it make?"

"Jaim," Delors said, "you're turning this into a very ugly trip by allowing yourself to become so bitter and—"

"Then get yourself a new partner when we get back," he told her, furious.

"You stubborn fool!" Delors said suddenly. "You silly little boy!"

Bridling, Jaim said, "Delors, you have no right to talk that way considering—"

"I have every right since I love you, Jaim."

The ovoid rushed on, filled with the discernible silence of all systems operating quite routinely. All systems, that is, except Jaim's.

"You what?" he said.

"I love you and therefore I care about what happens to you, and you'll be thrown back on the service occupation scrap heap if you keep defying the Monitors." To all those who ranged, those who did not were an unfortunate class apart. It was a forgivable arrogance, considering the risks of ranging.

"But the Monitors are so old!" Jaim retorted.

"Oh, Jaim."

"What's wrong? Why are you crying?"

"Because you're so addled in so many ways. It must be your age. Or your sex."

"Delors, I don't understand you."

"No, because you're a man. I said I love you."

"And I say that if you do, you ought to understand how I feel!"

"How about how I feel?" Delors answered.

But Jaim was angry, hardly hearing her, rushing on: "The Monitors cause the trouble. Why can't they understand the simple fact that I want to see farther than they are willing to permit—?"

The question at once became academic. Around the ovoid, *ping-pong-ping-pang*, a storm of the starry scarlet needles descended.

The needle-storm struck the ovoid's receptors with a fury twice that of the previous attack's. Jaim was thunderstruck:

"In this sector too? That's coincidentally impos—"

Academics once more, for the ovoid was smoking furiously, yawing and pitching. Deep within the relays Jaim felt a mounting input. The Monitors were preparing to take control and rescue them again.

Delors made whimpering sounds. The ovoid was incinerating at a rate twice as rapid as the first time, and Jaim could count the time left for him to do something in microfractions of a thought's flow.

"The overrides—?" Delors cried out through a wild interfering static.

"I'll try." Jaim immediately saw his own self in the Sleep, with the huge black stain washing down over what he surely knew would be his corpse.

"*The overrides—*" Delors cried again through the snapping

and rupturing of wires. The ovoid's surface was beginning to dance with a reddish halo. Bits flaked away.

Jaim tried to select the proper relays, rearranging, rethinking.

Fear, fear, it was all around him, black clouds of it. His wired mind hurt. *Fear.*

Jaim knew he must act.

Ping-pong-ping-pang, the fiery needles were eating the ovoid away.

Jaim knew he must. He knew he must. He knew he must. He thought, rearranging, reconnecting—

The input signals from the Monitors welled into the ovoid, but feebly. The powerdrain was barely perceptible.

I must, Jaim thought, a scream of thought. The black fear wrapped around the image of his own self in the Sleep, wiped it out, killed him—

He was dead.

Then how did he know he was dead?

He was *not* dead. His wired mind was still functioning within the crisping ovoid, amid the internal sparks, the rupturing microconnectors, the ozone reek. He had yet one infinite part of a thought's time to rethink the last curcuit with all his effort—

The sensory pandemonium, and Delors' shrieks, melted into the quickest of blacks.

Jaim was horrified when it all shifted into focus again. He was horrified and stunned because he realized he had defied the Monitors, choked the fear, and worked the overrides.

"Jaim, Jaim—"

"Delors, are you all right?"

"Yes, yes. Where are we? Where did you carry us?"

She sounded terrified, and had a perfect right. Frantically Jaim extended the optical stalks to take in the awful, crystalline brilliance of strange radiant galaxies which shone like the faces of a single gemstone. There were violent bursts of orange gas in the upper right quadrant and fierce, zagging streaks of yellow molten energy in the left central quadrant. Everything was so unfamiliar and terrifying and beautiful that Jaim could not encompass it all.

He realized he must compute the location. The second after

he had put in the request, the ovoid's storage banks, still functioning, relayed back a total absence of data.

"We don't know where we are," Jaim said.

They were alone. They were truly alone. They were so far out, the powerdrain had become but the barest of submerged tingles.

Yet there was still a flurry of signals. Despite his great fright, which mingled with a monstrous sense of awe at these sights so unlike anything he had ever seen or been trained to see, he responded with the right relay. The voiceless speech of the Monitors flowed in:

"Much honor, Jaim. Much honor, Delors. Much honor."

Was this some sickly trick of theirs before they punished him? Jaim said:

"I have overridden you."

"And jumped farther than any team has ever jumped from the 1201st of all Homes."

Delors said, "H—how far?"

A tone of pride channeled in from far behind: "A jump of five hundred twenty-two trillion light-years."

Even Jaim was staggered. Faintly he heard the Monitors congratulating themselves. There was an even heavier flurry of this sort of traffic, with Jaim only catching its leakage. He signaled and interrupted:

"Are you making a joke with me? I was restricted—"

"Deliberately, Jaim."

"Deliberately?"

"According to plan, Jaim."

"What plan? To what purpose?"

"Some lessons, Jaim," the voice went on—he knew suddenly it was Mordkye's—"cannot be taught in the text halls of our own Home. Chief among them is the seizure of the power which the minds of those who range hold while they are young. We are no longer young. The power had seeped out of us, as it will one day seep out of you. But we can teach, both by lesson and by ploy. The fiery needle storms are but projections. Real, oh yes. They could have killed you both times. But we are the projectors. In the first test we gave you, the first storm, your fear remained greater than the power of your own mind, Jaim. In our second test, you killed the fear and seized the power and used the relays we built expressly so that you could one day discover them and override because you wanted to override and not because we bade you override."

Jaim felt outraged. "A trick—!"

"A lesson," came the correction. "The last lesson. New to each team of those who range. Now you must pledge, Jaim and Delors, never to tell the lesson to any other new teams."

At once Delors replied, "Pledged."

"It is well," Mordkye said.

"But why a ploy?" Jaim demanded.

"Because even the minds of those who range, Jaim, are delicate things and, yes, primitive things in part. Where you are, the distances are vast and the splendors so awesome and new as to be of shattering power. We must know whether our teams, especially the controlling male, can survive or will be broken. Fear is the killer of the power to range far, but the fear can be killed provided we have chosen well. In you we have chosen well. Jump, Jaim, and plot after you jump in distances of your own choosing. We will watch but never command again. Only return to jump again, for only in this way is the dark pushed back and knowledge extended. Much honor, Jaim. Much honor, Delors. Much honor—"

Like a humming river of signals, all the Monitors flowed in: "Much honor."

"Jaim," Delors was saying, "I wish I had my body to cry, it's so beautiful. I wish I could cry real tears and feel them on my face."

Jaim felt gigantic. His optical stalks searched and he nearly forgot to turn on the image scanners as the ovoid wandered among the strange, burning starclusters beyond which, immensity upon immensity, fresh lights now gleamed. Lights and lights running away to the limit of all knowing—

But he would know. Yes, he would.

Jaim whooped. He understood it all. The test had come, been met, was gone. Never had the Monitors meant to hold him checked. Just the opposite. They had taught him to range as men were meant to range. He, Jaim.

Delors caught his thought, said joyously, though in a shy way, "Jaim? I am here."

"I'm glad," he said, as they readied to jump to the far, far lights.

Mind Out
of Time

.... by Keith Laumer

1

Strapped tight in the padded acceleration couch in the command cell of the Extrasolar Exploratory Module, Lieutenant Colonel Jake Vanderguerre tensed against the telltale bubbling sensation high in his chest, the light, tentative pinprick of an agony that could hurl itself against him like a white-hot anvil. The damned bootleg heart pills must be losing their punch; it had been less than six hours since he'd doped himself up for the mission. . . .

Beside him, Captain Lester Teal cocked a well-arched eyebrow at him. "You all right, Colonel?"

"I'm fine." Vanderguerre heard the ragged quality of his voice; to cover it, he nodded toward the ten-inch screen on which the clean-cut features of Colonel Jack Sudston of Mission Control on Luna glowed in enthusiastic color. "I wish the son of a bitch would cut the chatter. He makes me nervous."

Teal grunted. "Let Soapy deliver his commercial, Colonel," he said. "In a minute we'll get the line about the devoted personnel of UNSA; and there might even be time for a fast mention of Stella and Jo, the devoted little women standing by."

". . . report that the module is now in primary position, and in a G condition," Sudston was saying heartily. "Ready for the first manned test of the magnetic torsion powered vehicle." He smiled out of the screen; his eyes, fixed on an off-screen cue-card, did not quite meet Vanderguerre's. "Now let's have a word from Van and Les, live from the MTE module, in solar orbit, at four minutes and fifty-three seconds from jump."

Vanderguerre thumbed the XMIT button.

"Roj, Mission Control," he said. "Les and I are rarin' to go. She's a sweet little, uh, module, Jack. Quite a view from out here. We have Earth in sight, can just make out the crescent. As for Luna, you look mighty small from here, Jack. Not much brighter than good old Sirius. MTE module out."

"While we wait, Van and Les's words are flashing toward us at the speed of light." Sudston's voice filled the transmission lag. "And even at that fantastic velocity—capable of circling the world ten times in each second—it takes a full twenty-eight seconds for—but here's Van's carrier now . . ."

"Roj, Mission Control." Vanderguerre listened as his own transmission was repeat-beamed to the television audience watching back on Earth.

"Damn the stage machinery," he said. "We could have flipped the switches any time in the last two hours."

"But then Soapy wouldn't have been able to air the big spectacle live on prime time," Teal reminded him sardonically.

"Spectacle," Vanderguerre snorted. "A fractional percentage capability check. We're sitting on a power plant that can tap more energy in a second than the total consumption of the human race through all previous history. And what do we do with it? Another baby step into space."

"Relax, Colonel." Teal quirked the corner of his mouth upward. "You wouldn't want to risk men's lives with premature experimentation, would you?"

"Ever heard of Columbus?" Vanderguerre growled. "Or the Wright boys, or Lindbergh?"

"Ever heard of a guy named Cocking?" Teal countered. "Back in the 1800s he built a parachute out of wicker. Went up in a balloon and tried it. It didn't work. I remember the line in the old newspaper I saw: 'Mister Cocking was found in a field at Lea, literally dashed to bits.' "

"I take my hat off to Mr. Cocking," Vanderguerre said. "He tried."

"There hasn't been a fatality directly attributable to the Program in the sixty-nine years since Lunar Station One," Teal said. "You want to be the first to louse up a no-hitter?"

Vanderguerre snorted a laugh. "I was the first man on Callisto, Teal. Did you know that? It's right there in the record— along with the baseball statistics and the mean annual rainfall at Centralia, Kansas. That was eighteen years ago." He put out a hand, ran it over the polished curve of the control mushroom. "So what if she blew up in our faces?" he said as if to himself. "Nobody lives forever."

". . . fifty-three seconds and counting," Sudston's voice chanted into the silence that followed Vanderguerre's remark. "The monitor board says—yes, it's coming down now, it's condition G all the way, the mission *is* go, all systems are clocking down without a hitch, a tribute to the expertise of the devoted personnel of UNSA, at minus forty-eight seconds and counting. . . ."

Teal twisted his head against the restraint of his harness to eye Vanderguerre.

"Don't mind me, kid," the older man said. "We'll take our little toad-hop, wait ten minutes for the tapes to spin, and duck back home for our pat on the head like good team men."

"Fifteen seconds and counting," Sudston's voice intoned. "Fourteen seconds. Thirteen . . ."

The two men's hands moved in a sure, trained sequence: READY lever down and locked. ARM lever down and locked.

". . . Four. Three. Two. One. Jump."

In unison, the men slammed home the big, paired, white-painted switches. There was a swiftly rising hum, a sense of mounting pressure . . .

2

Teal shook off the dizziness that had swirled him like a top as the torsion drive hurled the tiny vessel outward into Deep Space; he gripped the chair arms, fighting back the nausea and anxiety that always accompanied the climactic moment of a shot.

It's all right, he told himself fiercely. *Nothing can go wrong. In three hours you'll be back aboard UNSA Nine, with half-a-dozen medics taping your belly growls. Relax . . .*

He forced himself to lean back in the chair; closed his eyes, savoring the familiarity of it, the security of the enclosing titanium-foam shell.

It was okay now. He knew what to do in any conceivable emergency. Just follow the routine. It was as simple as that. That was the secret he'd learned long ago, when he had first realized that the military life was the one for him; the secret that had given him his reputation for coolness in the face of danger: Courage consisted of knowing what to do.

He opened his eyes, scanned instrument faces with swift, trained precision, turned to Vanderguerre. The senior officer looked pale, ill.

"Forty-two million miles out, give or take half a million," Teal said. "Elapsed time, point oh, oh, oh seconds."

"Mama mia," Vanderguerre breathed. "We're sitting on a live one, boy!"

The voice issuing from the command was a whispery crackle.

"*. . . that the module is now in primary position, and in a G condition,*" Sudston's distance-distorted image was saying. "*Ready for the first manned test of the magnetic torsion powered vehicle. . . .*"

"We passed up Soapy's transmission," Teal said.

"By God, Teal," Vanderguerre said. "I wonder what she'll do. What she'll *really* do!"

Teal felt his heart begin to *thump-ump, thump-ump.* He sensed what was coming as he looked at Vanderguerre. Vanderguerre looked back, eyeing him keenly. Was there a calculating look there, an assessing? Was he wondering about Teal, about his famous reputation for guts?

"What you said before about spotting the record." Vanderguerre's voice was level, casual. "Is that really the way you feel, Les?"

"You're talking about deviating from the programmed mission?" Teal kept his voice steady.

"We'd have to unlock from auto-sequencing and reprogram," Vanderguerre said. "It would be four minutes before Soapy knew anything. They couldn't stop us."

"Roj, Lunar Control," Vanderguerre's voice crackled, relayed from the moon. *"Les and I are rarin' to go. . . ."*

"The controls are interlocked," Vanderguerre added. "We'd have to do it together." His eyes met Teal's, held them for a moment, turned away.

"Forget it," he said quickly. "You're young, you've got a career ahead, a family. It was a crazy idea—"

"I'll call your bluff," Teal cut him off harshly. "I'm game."

Say no, a voice inside him prayed. *Say no, and let me off the hook . . .*

Vanderguerre's tongue touched his lips; he nodded.

"Good for you, kid. I didn't think you had it in you."

3

"I've locked the guidance system on Andromeda," Vanderguerre said. The pain was still there, lurking—and the jump hadn't helped any. But it would hold off a little while, for this. It *had* to . . .

"How much power?" Teal asked.

"All of it," Vanderguerre said. "We'll open her up. Let's see what she'll do."

Teal punched keys, coding instructions into the panel.

". . . UNSA Station Nine has just confirmed the repositioning of the double-X module in Martian orbit." The excited voice of Colonel Sudston was suddenly louder, clearer, as the big Lunar transmitter beam swung to the center of the new position of the experimental craft. "Van, let's hear from you!"

"You'll hear from us," Vanderguerre said. "You'll hear plenty."

"Board set up," Teal said formally. "Ready for jump, sir."

"Van and Les have their hands full right now, carrying out the planned experiments aboard the MTE vehicle," the voice from the screen chattered. "They're two lonely men at this moment, over forty million miles from home . . ."

"Last chance to change your mind," Vanderguerre said.

"You can back out if you want to," Teal said tightly.

"Jump," Vanderguerre said. Two pairs of hands flipped the

switch sequence. A whine rose to a wire-thin hum. There was a sense of pressure that grew and grew . . .

Blackout dropped over Vanderguerre like a steel door.

4

This time, Teal realized, was worse—much worse. Under him, the seat lifted, lifted, pivoting back and endlessly over. Nausea stirred in him, brought a clammy film to his forehead. His bones seemed to vibrate in resonance to the penetrating keening of the torsion drive.

Then, abruptly, stillness. Teal drew a deep breath, opened his eyes. The command screen was blank, lit only by the darting flicker of random noise. The instruments—

Teal stared, rigid in shock. The MP scale read zero; the navigation fix indicator hunted across the grid aimlessly; the R counter registered negative. It didn't make sense. The jump must have blown every breaker in the module. Teal glanced up at the direct-vision dome.

Blackness, unrelieved, immense.

Teal's hands moved in an instinctive gesture to reset the controls for the jump back to the starting point; he caught himself, turned to Vanderguerre.

"Something's fouled up. Our screens are out—" He broke off. Vanderguerre lay slack in the elaborately equipped chair, his mouth half open, his face the color of candle wax.

"Vanderguerre!" Teal slipped his harness, grabbed for the other's wrist. There was no discernible pulse.

Sweat trickled down into the corner of Teal's eye.

"Interlocked controls," he said. "Jake, you've got to wake up. I can't do it alone. You hear me, Jake? Wake up!" He shook the flaccid arm roughly. Vanderguerre's head lolled. Teal crouched to scan the life-system indicators on the unconscious man's shoulder repeater. The heartbeat was weak, irregular, the respiration shallow. He was alive—barely.

Teal half fell back into his chair. He forced himself to breathe deep, again, and again. Slowly, the panic drained away.

Okay. They'd pulled a damn-fool stunt, and something had gone wrong. A couple of things. But that didn't mean everything wasn't going to come out all right, if he just kept his head, followed the rules.

First, he had to do something about Vanderguerre. He unclipped the highly sophisticated medkit from its niche, forcing himself to move carefully, deliberately, remembering his training. One by one he attached the leads of the diagnostic monitor to Vanderguerre's suit-system contacts.

Fourteen minutes later, Vanderguerre stirred and opened his eyes.

"You blacked out," Teal said quickly, then checked himself. "How do you feel?" He forced his tone level.

"I'm . . . all right. What . . . ?"

"We made the jump. Something went wrong. Screens are out; comlink too."

"How . . . far?"

"I don't know, I tell you!" Teal caught the hysterical note in his voice, clamped his teeth hard. "I don't know," he repeated in a calmer tone. "We'll jump back now. All we have to do is backtrack on reverse settings—" He realized he was talking to reassure himself, cut off abruptly.

"Got to determine . . . our position," Vanderguerre panted. "Otherwise—wasted."

"To hell with that," Teal snapped. "You're a sick man," he added. "You need medical attention."

Vanderguerre was struggling to raise his head far enough to see the panel.

"Instruments are acting crazy," Teal said. "We've got to—"

"You've checked out the circuits?"

"Not yet. I was busy with you." Silently Teal cursed the defensiveness of his tone.

"Check 'em."

Teal complied, tight-lipped.

"All systems G," he reported.

"All right," Vanderguerre said, his voice weak but calm. "Circuits hot, but the screens show nothing. Must be something masking 'em. Let's take a look. Deploy the direct-vision scopes."

Teal's hands shook as he swung his eyepiece into position. He swore silently, adjusted the instrument. A palely glowing rectangular grid, angled sharply outward, filled the viewfield: one of the module's out-flung radiation surfaces. The lens, at least, was clear. But why the total blackness of the sky beyond? He tracked past the grid. A glaringly luminous object swam into view, oblong, misty, and nebulous in outline.

"I've got something," he said. "Off the port fan."

He studied the oval smear of light—about thirty inches in width, he estimated, and perhaps a hundred feet distant.

"Take a look to starboard," Vanderguerre said. Teal shifted the scope, picked up a second object, half again as large as the first. Two smaller, irregularly shaped objects hung off to one side. Squinting against the glare, Teal adjusted the scope's filter. The bright halo obscuring the larger object dimmed. Now he could make out detail, a pattern of swirling, clotted light, curving out in two spiral arms from a central nucleus—

The realization of what he was seeing swept over Teal with a mind-numbing shock.

5

Vanderguerre stared at the shape of light, the steel spike in his chest almost, for the moment, forgotten.

Andromeda—and the Greater and Lesser Magellanic Clouds. And the other, smaller one: the Milky Way, the home galaxy.

"What the hell!" Teal's harsh voice jarred at him. "Even if we're halfway to Andromeda—a million light-years—it should only subtend a second or so of arc! That thing looks like you could reach out and touch it!"

"Switch on the cameras, Les," he whispered. "Let's get a record—"

"Let's get out of here, Vanderguerre!" Teal's voice was ragged. "My God, I never thought—"

"Nobody did." Vanderguerre spoke steadily. "That's why we've got to tape it all, Les—"

"We've got enough! Let's go back! Now!"

Vanderguerre looked at Teal. The younger man was pale, wild-eyed. He was badly shaken. But you couldn't blame him. A million lights in one jump. So much for the light barrier, gone the way of the sound barrier.

"Now," Teal repeated. "Before . . ."

"Yeah," Vanderguerre managed. "Before you find yourself marooned with a corpse. You're right. Okay. Set it up."

He lay slackly in the chair. His chest seemed swollen to giant size, laced across with vivid arcs of agony that pulsed like muffled explosions. Any second now. The anvil was teetering, ready to fall. And the dual controls required two men to jump the module back along her course line. There was no time to waste.

"Board set up," Teal snapped. "Ready for jump."

Vanderguerre raised his hands to the controls; the steel spike drove into his chest.

"Jump," he gasped, and slammed the levers down—

The white-hot anvil struck him with unbearable force.

6

Teal shook his head, blinked the fog from before his eyes; avidly, he scanned the panel.

Nothing had changed. The instruments still gave their dataless readings; the screen was blank.

"Vanderguerre—it didn't work—" Teal felt a sudden constriction, like a rope around his throat, as he stared at the motionless figure in the other chair.

"Jake!" he shouted. "You can't be dead! Not yet! I'd be stuck here! Jake! Wake up! Wake up!" As from a great distance, he heard his own voice screaming; but he was powerless to stop it. . . .

7

From immense depths, Vanderguerre swam upward, to surface on a choppy sea of pain. He lay for a while, fighting for breath, his mind blanked of everything except the second-to-second struggle for survival. After a long time, the agony eased; with an effort, he turned his head.

Teal's seat was empty.

8

What did it mean? Vanderguerre asked himself for the twentieth time. What had happened? They'd jumped, he'd felt the drive take hold—

And Teal. Where the hell was Teal? He couldn't have left the module; it was a sealed unit. Nothing could leave it, not even wastes, until the techs at UNSA Nine cut her open. . . .

But he was gone. And out there, Andromeda still loomed, big as a washtub, and the Milky Way. It was impossible, all of it. Even the jump. Was it all a dream, a dying fancy?

No. Vanderguerre rejected the idea. *Something's happened here. Something I don't understand—not yet. But I've got data—a little data, anyway. And I've got a brain. I've got to look at the situation, make some deductions, decide on a course of action.*

From somewhere, a phrase popped into Vanderguerre's mind:

"Space is a property of matter. . . ."

And where there was no matter, there would be . . . spacelessness.

"Sure," Vanderguerre whispered. "If we'd stopped to think, we'd have realized there's no theoretical limit to the MTE. We opened her up all the way—and the curve went off the graph. It threw us right out of the galaxy, into a region where the matter density is one ion per cubic light. All the way to the end of space: dead end. No wonder we didn't go any farther —or that we can't jump back. Zero is just a special case of infinity. And that's as far as we'd go, if we traveled on forever. . . ."

His eye fell on Teal's empty seat. *Yeah—so far so good. But what about Teal? How does the Vanderguerre theory of negative space explain that one . . . ?*

Abruptly, fire flickered in Vanderguerre's chest. He stiffened, his breath cut off in his throat. So much for theories. This was it. No doubt about it. Three times and out. Strange that it had to end this way, so far away, in space and time, from everything he'd ever loved.

The vise in Vanderguerre's chest closed; the flames leaped higher, consuming the universe in raging incandescence. . . .

9

Vanderguerre was standing on a graveled path beside a lake. It was dawn, and a chill mist lay over the water. Beyond the hazy line of trees on the far side, a hill rose, dotted with buildings. He recognized the scene at once: Lake Beryl. And the date: May 1, 2007. It all came back to him as clearly as if it had been only yesterday, instead of twenty years. The little skiers' hotel, deserted now in summer, the flowers on the table, the picnic lunch packed in a basket by the waiter, with the bottle of vin rosé poking out under the white napkin. . . .

And Mirla. He knew, before he turned, that she would be standing there, smiling as he had remembered her, down through the years. . . .

10

The music was loud, and Teal raised his glass for a refill, glad of the noise, of the press of people, of the girl who clung close beside him, her breasts firm and demanding against him.

For a moment, a phantom memory of another place seemed to pluck at Teal's mind—an urgent vision of awful loneliness, of a fear that overwhelmed him like a breaking wave— He pushed the thought back.

Wine sloshed from the glass. It didn't matter. Teal drank deep, let the glass fall from his hand, turned, sought the girl's mouth hungrily.

11

"Van—is anything wrong?" Mirla asked. Her smile had changed to a look of concern.

"No. Nothing," Vanderguerre managed. *Hallucination!* a voice inside his head said. *And yet it's real—as real as ever life was real. . . .*

Mirla put her hand on his arm, looking up into his face.

"You stopped so suddenly—and you look . . . worried."

"Mirla . . . something strange has happened." Vanderguerre's eyes went to the bench beside the path. He led her to it, sank down on it. His heart was beating strongly, steadily.

"What is it, Van?"

"A dream? Or . . . is this the dream?"

"Tell me."

Vanderguerre did.

"I was there," he finished. "Just the wink of an eye ago. And now—I'm here."

"It's a strange dream, Van. But after all—it *is* just a dream. And this is real."

"Is it, Mirla? Those years of training, were they a dream? I still know how to dock a Mark Nine on nine ounces of reaction mass. I know the math—the smell of the coolant when a line breaks under high G—the names of the men who put the first marker on Pluto, the first party who landed on Ceres, and—"

"Van—it was just a dream! You dreamed those things—"

"What date is this?" he cut in.

"May first—"

"May first, two-oh oh-seven. The date the main dome at Mars Station One blew and killed twelve tech personnel. One of them was Mayfield, the agronomist!" Vanderguerre jumped to his feet. "I haven't seen a paper, Mirla. You know that. We've been walking all night."

"You mean—you think—"

"Let's find a paper. The news should be breaking any time now!"

They went up the path, across the park, crossed an empty street; ten minutes later, from the open door of an all-night dinomat, a television blared:

". . . just received via Bellerophon relay. Among the dead are Colonel Mark Spencer, Marsbase Commandant—"

"An error," Vanderguerre put in. "He was hurt, but recovered."

". . . Doctor Gregor Mayfield, famed for his work in desert ecology . . ."

"Mayfield!" Mirla gasped. "Van—you knew!"

"Yes." Vanderguerre's voice was suddenly flat. "In the absence of matter, space doesn't exist. Time is a function of space; it's the medium in which events happen. With no space, there can be no movement—and no time. All times become the same. I can be there—or here . . ."

"Van!" Mirla clung to his arm. "I'm frightened! What does it mean?"

"I've got to go back."

"Go . . . back?"

"Don't you see, Mirla? I can't desert my ship, my co-pilot —abandon the program I gave my life to. I can't let them chalk up the MTE as a failure—a flop that killed two men! It would kill the last feeble spark that's keeping the program going!"

"I don't understand, Van. How can you—go back—to a dream?"

"I don't know, Mirla. But I've got to. Got to try." He disengaged his arm, looked down into her face.

"Forgive me, Mirla. A miracle happened here. Maybe . . ." Still looking into her face, he closed his eyes, picturing the command cell aboard the MTE, remembering the pressure of the seat harness across his body, the vertigo of weightlessness, the smell of the cramped quarters, the pain. . . .

12

. . . the pain thrust at him like a splintered lance. He opened his eyes, saw the empty chair, the blank screens.

"Teal," he whispered. "Where are you, Teal?"

13

Teal looked up. An old man was pushing through the crowd toward the table.

"Come with me, Teal," the old man said.

"Go to hell!" Teal snarled. "Get away from me, I don't know you and I don't want to know you!"

"Come with me, Teal—"

Teal leaped to his feet, caught up the wine bottle, smashed it down over the old man's head. He went down; the crowd drew back; a woman screamed. Teal stared down at the body. . . .

. . . he was at the wheel of a car, a low-slung, hard-sprung powerhouse that leaped ahead under his foot, faster, faster. The road unreeled before him, threading its way along the flank of a mountain. Ahead, tendrils of mist obscured the way. Suddenly, there was a man there, in the road, holding up his hand. Teal caught a glimpse of a stern, lined face, gray hair—

The impact threw the man fifty feet into the air. Teal saw the body plummet down among the treetops of the slope below the road in the same instant that the veering car plunged through the guardrail . . .

. . . the music from the ballroom was faint, here on deck. Teal leaned against the rail, watching the lights of Lisboa sliding away across the mirrored water.

"It's beautiful, Les," the slim, summer-gowned woman beside him said. "I'm glad I came. . . ."

An old man came toward Teal, walking silently along the deck.

"Come with me, Teal," he said. "You've got to come back."

"No!" Teal recoiled. "Stay away, damn you! I'll never come back!"

"You've got to, Teal," the grim old man said. "You can't forget."

"Vanderguerre," Teal whispered hoarsely, "I left you there —in the module—sick, maybe dying. Alone."

"We've got to take her back, Teal. You and I are the only ones who know. We can't let it all go, Teal. We owe the program that much."

"To hell with the program," Teal snarled. "But you. I forgot about you, Jake. I swear I forgot."

"Let's go back now, Les."

Teal licked his lips. He looked at the slim girl, standing, her knuckles pressed against her face, staring at him. His eyes went back to Vanderguerre.

"I'm coming of my own free will, Jake," he said. "I ran— but I came back. Tell them that."

14

"Not . . . much time . . ." Vanderguerre whispered as he lay slack in the chair. "Enough . . . for one more . . . try. Out here . . . the MTE can't do it . . . alone. We . . . have to help."

Teal nodded. "I know. I couldn't put it in words, but I know."

"Solar orbit," Vanderguerre whispered. "One microsecond after jump."

"Jake—it just hit me! The jump will kill you!"

"Prepare for jump." Vanderguerre's voice was barely audible. "Jump!"

Their hands went out; levers slammed home. Mighty forces gripped the universe, twisted it inside out.

15

"*. . . that the module is now in primary position, and in a G condition,*" the faint voice of Colonel Sudston crackled from the screen.

Teal looked across at Vanderguerre. The body lay at peace, the features smiling faintly.

Teal depressed the XMIT button. "MTE to Mission Control," he said. "Jump completed. And I have the tragic honor to report the death of Lieutenant Colonel Jacob Vanderguerre in the line of duty. . . ."

16

. . . he knew, before he turned, that she would be standing there, smiling as he had remembered her, down through the years.

"Van—is anything wrong?" Mirla asked.

"Nothing," Vanderguerre said. "Nothing in this universe."

The Inspector

by James McKimmey

The planet of Tnp, a name settled upon by its citizens to celebrate their insatiable desire to be The New People, was a small, hazily defined globe when our pilot, Stoke, saw him. "Right portview," he said, shoving thumb and forefinger in that direction.

Benny Quick moved his stocky body over there, and I followed. We looked through the wide window of our compact ship, called the *Wardben*, into that cold vacuum of space. Our powerful finder-spot washed the figure with merciless light. A white flier suit encased his body. His thruster was strapped to his back, but it was not in use—he was simply in orbit. I saw that his face-window had fogged, then frozen from the inside, so that we couldn't see his features. He was dead, and had become an orbiting statue of what had once been a handsome twenty-three-year-old Steven Terry, special pride of Tnp.

I looked closely at the oxygen tube attached to the front of his suit. "What do you think, Benny?"

Benny shrugged. "Who knows?"

"Let's put it down," I said to Stoke.

The giant landing flat of Sovell, capital city of Tnp, was wet with recent rain when Benny Quick, Stoke, and I went down the walkway from the ship. Because of the reddish nature of the planet's general terrain and the early sunlight striking the moisture-laden atmosphere, the long slug-shaped car of the First Minister, Thor Prinz, rested at the edge of the flat in an orange gloom.

There was no regaling reception committee, only Prinz, whom I recognized by his long white hair blowing wispily in the wet breeze, and two others—probably security.

"Mister Warden Forest?" he asked.

I shook his limp hand in response, seeing fatigue in his soft face and weariness in his very flat-silver eyes. "This is my assistant, Mister Quick," I said. "My pilot, Mister Stoke."

With that brief formality away, Benny and I left Stoke, who would remain at the flat, and got into the back seat of the car, facing Prinz. Prinz remained silent as the vehicle rolled silently away on its slot-track, accelerating to five hundred miles per hour. The speed prevented a thorough inspection of the Tnpian architecture. Buildings became merely orange-white blurs. But I had, using films and still pictures, studied the general building lines of the planet in New York before leaving Earth. As a sixty-year-old civilization founded on a planet rich in natural resources, specializing in turning those resources into expert manufacturing, the emphasis had been on simplicity.

The car slowed, its track taking it in a curl to stop in front of the First Minister's rectangular, marble-white headquarters house. He sat watching me with those flat-silver eyes, which were nearly the same color as his simple skin-tight, one-piece suit, usual apparel for male Tnpians.

"After you, Mister Forest," he said tonelessly.

"Thank you, sir."

In a broad room created with the same lack of complication that characterized the exterior, Benny and I sat with Prinz. Chairs were made of white stone, sculpted to hold the body comfortably. Walls were plain. Windows were draped with heavy white material. Prinz, in his pale suit, his eyes troubled, and frothy hair billowing, looked as an ancient Greek leader in modern dress might—which was natural enough, I thought; Tnp was going through a Greek phase of some consequence.

"An Inspector," he said, not quite hiding his irritation and anger.

"We were formed to help new colonies, Mister Minister. That is our purpose—no other."

"It's interference!"

Benny, who appeared to have been bundled much too hurriedly into his soft green flight uniform, bent his head, red hair tousled; he stared patiently at his low black boots—we were quite used to this kind of response from heads of relatively new colonies.

"We would like," I said quietly, "to create as much good will as possible. We only hope that you will find it acceptable to cooperate with us."

"We have nearly a million people on this planet! Why is one individual—?"

"Why is one individual left orbiting in that fashion?" I finished pointedly.

Prinz held his breath for a moment, then sighed tiredly.

"Steven Terry," I said.

"That was his name," Prinz said with some indication of sarcasm.

"How did he get up there, Mister Minister?"

Prinz looked at me again, with antagonism. "He simply took one of our new T53 ships up on a pleasure flight. He placed it in orbit, then got out of the ship for a thrust-swim. He was an expert flier, an expert swimmer, as you probably know. It was recreation. Nothing more!"

"But something happened. What?"

Prinz shrugged defiantly. "It hasn't been ascertained."

"He's been up there for two weeks."

"Is there any *harm* in that, Mister Forest? He's frozen, quite well preserved. Why does Earth Security *care*, sir!"

I rested a hand on a knee and looked at my large-knuckled fingers. Minister Thor Prinz knew why, of course. Trained as completely as I was by the Special Investigation Section of the Earth Security Council and aided by an expert handyman such as Benny Quick, I was ready to check on a malfunction, no matter how small, in the national affairs of any of the dozens of Earth-colonized planets that had not yet achieved independent franchises. The planet colony of Tnp would not earn its franchise for another forty years. It was subject to this sort of scrutiny, because Tnp possessed the usual array of weapons that could, with wrong intention, create devastation in the galaxy. It was true that citizens of Tnp were as subject to dying as citizens anywhere else, including by means of accident. But when a man died in space, as Steven Terry had done, he was not usually left in orbit.

"Do you think it was accidental?" I asked.

"He was observed after audio contact with him failed. The look of his face then would indicate that he died from lack of oxygen."

"Mechanical failure?"

Prinz sat motionless in his stone chair and gazed at nothing. He did not appear remotely plebeian; he looked to be a highly intelligent leader who had governed his electorate with sensitivity, authority, and zeal. He was approaching seventy-eight years, and he had been elected to the highest political post obtainable on Tnp for three consecutive six-year terms, the last of which, according to Earth's calendar, would end in four months.

"You don't know what killed him," I said. "Yet there has been no specific investigation of the matter?"

"Possibly," Prinz said slowly, "it was an act of God."

I looked at Benny's weathered, creased face, seeing his lids droop in a fashion that others might have mistaken for inattention or boredom or possibly sleepiness. But I knew Benny. We had covered assignments together ranging from the highly dangerous to those requiring an ultimate in patience and tact; I recognized precisely how his very alert mind was turning.

"Tell me about Steven Terry," I said to the First Minister.

"You don't have that information on file in New York?"

"I'd like to hear it from you, sir."

Prinz stood up and moved about the room, looking at me frequently. "He was one of our finest young people. One of our absolutely finest!"

"How did he come to be that way, sir?"

"Ah!" He shook his head impatiently. "How could you understand our culture, Mister Forest? How possibly?"

"I've been educated very definitely in that direction. I have considerable experience with a collection of cultures among the various colony planets. I might add that you, Mister Minister, were born on Earth, after all."

"I was eighteen years old when I came here, Mister Forest —sixty years ago. I know nothing now but the life of a Tnpian. I am afraid that is what you will not comprehend!"

"Let me try, sir."

He returned to his chair and sat down, stretching one slim leg forward, bending the other at the knee, in a classic pose.

"Steven Terry is a second-generation Tnpian." He made the simple statement with stress, the tone of his voice creating obvious importance.

I nodded.

"You must understand that, sir. *That* is what is involved with this."

I felt relieved, yet more intense, now that it seemed his defenses were breaking down in the face of the reality that Steven Terry had once been.

"He was born to young parents in the Ziwig Plains," Prinz went on. "His father was a construction laborer involved in the establishment of one of our largest factories located in that area. His mother had five other children. All of them were killed by red-dust poisoning in that regrettable storm of nineteen years ago—all, that is, except young Terry, who was left parentless at the age of four. He was placed in one of our Institute Parentries."

Prinz's expression became one of detached, slight pain. The Institute Parentries had turned out to be less than successful experiments in the lives of Tnpians. The units had been run in precise terms, using mechanical audio and visio developments to reproduce a supposed ideal environment for parentless children. All that had been lacking, in an otherwise perfect idyll of machine-taught perfection, had been a human quality. It had been to Prinz's credit that he had led the fight to close them, which he had accomplished during his fifth year in office. The Tnpian culture had since adapted a simplified teacher-counselor system for bringing up orphans, which had proved far more satisfactory, despite obvious drawbacks. Yet, I reminded myself Steven Terry, the young hero, had been an early product of one of those mechanized Institute Parentries.

"At the age of nine," Prinz continued, "he was transferred into one of the new teacher-counselor homes, where he displayed astonishing capabilities which had not been detected in those mechanized failures of Institute Parentries. His I.Q. was precisely 180. He was extraordinarily coordinated. He owned a perfect musical ear. I am proud of the teacher-counselor developments we have made here on Tnp, Mister Forest. Within three years, under proper guidance, Steven Terry became a celebrated figure in our civilization."

"At the age of twelve."

"Precisely," Prinz said, his eyes bright. "He began appearing on television screens all over the planet. First, as a child intellectual. He was able to quote from every classic written through the twenty-first century. He was not simply a memory instrument; he could *think*. He debated some of our best scholars and made them taste defeat. Moreover—"

"He was a skilled electronic harpist."

"Quite right. A prodigy. You must understand that here we strive for the complete man. That is the ultimate ideal."

"Steven Terry was also a superb athlete."

"Six years ago, when he was seventeen, he swept our Greek Games with his prowess in virtually every competition in which he participated."

"All of that made him a colony hero."

"Untarnished, unblemished."

"Now he is grieved throughout Tnp?"

"Obviously," Prinz said, a metallic note of derision in his voice.

"Who grieves him most, Mister Minister?"

"The planet at large, sir."

"Wasn't there a girl?"

"Of course, there was a girl—Reecie Adams. Another of our finest Tnpian youths. They were engaged to be married. It was that romance which absolutely solidified the aura of rightness about Steven Terry into the mind of virtually every citizen. From the pain, the anguish, the terror, the commonplace drudgery of everyday life for most of our citizens—and I've never said Tnp is a paradise, Mister Forest; there are no paradises in our galactic existence—Steven Terry and Reecie Adams stood out in bold relief. Steven had the looks of a classic athlete. Reecie is an extraordinarily beautiful girl, skilled, talented as well—one of our best pilots, as Steven Terry was. It was the romance of romances, in our sixty-year-old history. Now—" His slim shoulders sagged under his tight suit.

He was giving me forthright facts, I thought, but he was continuing to evade the honest and important question: Why had Steven Terry been left in orbit?

"*I* formed the leadership to outlaw the Institute Parentries, Mister Forest," he said to me, a note of imploring edging into his voice. "*I* was the force behind creating the new teacher-counselor homes."

He was, I realized with surprise, pleading to me about that seemingly incidental point. But it was, I decided, only a continuation of his evasiveness.

"Where will we find rooms, Mister Minister?" I asked, suddenly weary.

"Here, if you wish," he said. "Or at the quarters at the landing flat, where your pilot is staying."

"I appreciate your hospitality, sir. The landing-flat quarters will be extremely suitable. We won't be in your way there."

He stood up as I did, looking at me intently. "You will have a car and chauffeur at your disposal, as well as a small flying craft. Look about our small world, Mister Forest. See what is happening. Feel the mood. Let this civilization of ours permeate your sensibilities. I will not impede your efforts in any way. But do not judge quickly. Do not come to the quick and obvious conclusions." He nodded briefly, eyes turning opaque. "Good morning, Mister Forest."

Stoke, Benny, and I were given three adjoining rooms in the sweeping quarters at the edge of the landing flat. My room offered a long-surfaced desk, equipped with visio-phone; I arranged my files brought here from Earth. Stoke and Benny had come in and were sitting quietly. Stoke, gangling and sardonic-looking, stretched indolently. When he was not flying the *Wardben*, he was indolent. But I had collected my small team with personal bias. If Stoke was nothing else, he was a pilot of any ship. That's where I used him.

"Anything I can do?" he asked now, yawning.

"Take it easy."

"Good." He stood up and ambled silently from the room.

Benny watched me shuffle through various cards and

papers. His forte was technical; he could observe the exterior of any sort of mechanical contrivance and sense if so much as a fuse were going. My own task was that of hound and psychologist. I tracked relentlessly. When I had covered enough field, I was required to stitch the facts I had nosed out into some fabric of understanding, always in human terms. I needed Benny to interpret the mechanical facts of life, where I could not. Yet he had achieved enough overall experience that he often added to his value by representing a sounding board for my own deductions.

"What?" Benny asked, instinctively following my direction of thought.

"The First Minister suggested that what killed Steven Terry might have been an act of God."

"You want my religious thoughts?"

"I want to know what you think about his statement."

"He was begging the point."

I nodded. "Run down the routine Steven Terry went through before going up. The check system. Equipment. All of it."

"Right." Benny nodded, and left.

I sorted through the collection of material I'd brought from New York. Finally I drew forth a pair of dimensional photographs. One was of Steven Terry.

His blond hair was clipped short against his well-molded head. His features were in clean, regular conformation. His skin was unusually pale for an outdoors participant. His eyes were pale blue, brightened with the drive and enthusiasm of youth. His neck created the straight lines of an athlete. He was of distinct Anglo-Saxon heritage, an amalgamation of blood lines that had created a singular Nordic look, known many years before.

Then I studied the picture of the girl, Reecie Adams. Here, I realized, was a suffusion of all Earth bloods streaming together, to produce a dazzlingly attractive young woman. Her skin was coffee-dark; there was the faintest trace of a Negroid flare in the nostrils of her narrow, small nose. Her forehead was broad and sloped upward to a wealth of shining black hair. Her mouth was wide and full-lipped, creating an immediate sexual response. Her eyes were black and heated, their almond shape showing the influence of a slight oriental ancestry. If I knew anything at all about human motives, there should have been within the now-dead Steven Terry some drive in his existence that had been created by this girl.

But I decided that I would see her only when I had circled the entire range of other possibilities.

I slid a capsule-background card forward to read a short summary of a man named Loren Hagen:

"Strongest politico-influence in Tnp. Base-roots influence. Behind-scenes manipulator, always. Original force behind First Minister Prinz. Loyalty based on practicality, if not opportunity. Splinter-opposition target. Solidly situated."

The selector dial of the visio-phone was installed at the right edge of the desk; the viewer was framed into the wall just at eye level. I pressed a combination of letters to create Hagen's code name and waited while the computer went to work. If I were not, as the result of local orders, to contact Hagen, the call would not go through. But moments later the viewer screen lighted. I looked at his rotund, florid image; his eyes stared back at me with the shrewd, calculating look of all professional political participants as they had looked for hundreds of years.

"Good morning, Mister Forest," he said in a rumbling, grating voice. "I've been expecting you."

"May I see you in person, sir?"

"At one? Your chauffeur will know where to find me."

At mid-morning, I stepped out into the clearing air, feeling warmth from the small rising sun. The air contained a peculiar sweet smell; I realized that it was from the abundant growth of avlopane, the prolifically growing flower common to the Sovell area of Tnp. A blossoming blue bank of them ran along the white side of the building from which I had just exited.

My chauffeur, named Harold, waited in the car assigned to me. He did not see me approaching; I looked through a window to see that he was watching a small screen just above his control board. Cameras were focused upon the orbiting body of Steven Terry speeding through space high above the planet. Finally Harold noticed me and got out quickly to let me into the section behind his seat.

125

I settled in and said, as he got behind the control board again, "Who's monitoring him, Harold?"

Harold turned, a thin, pinched-faced man with a humble expression. "Carry him all the time, around Tnp. All stations. Mourning period."

"I see."

"Shame."

"Yes, it is."

"Something went wrong. Don't know what. Fate, I guess. He was something, that Terry."

"You've been on Tnp quite a while, Harold?"

"Going on ten years. I come from New York. Bronx."

"Miss it?"

"Not me. Did, in the beginning. But I think back on it, and it ain't what I got here. This is the new world, Mister Forest. This is where I put my roots. Married a Tnpian girl. Got three kids now. You couldn't force me back to that Bronx now. This is mine, here. Place like this, if it breeds somebody like Steven Terry going around up there, that's a good place to be. Damned shame it went wrong for him. *Couldn't* have been his fault. He was too good. Had to be fate. The gods said it was so, and there he is dead, shooting around."

"Gods?" I asked.

"Well, God, gods, whatever. You know what I mean."

"Perhaps I do," I said, not at all certain of the validity of that response. "I want to see Loren Hagen at one o'clock. In the meantime, just drive me around the city."

The car sped into the central section of the city, where I got out and walked along a quiet avenue running between commercial stores. Dozens of Tnpians were standing outside doorways, looking into the sky with tubular instruments to their eyes. I recalled the highly developed binoculars that had been perfected on this planet; I knew that they were watching Steven Terry's body. I stepped into several stores to find that countless television screens were allowing clusters of people to watch that body speeding through space.

I spoke casually to several. They looked at my Earthian flight suit with little interest; commerce was heavy between Tnp and Earth, and, in their eyes, there was nothing unusual about my dress. All of them replied that it was a time of mourning. When I asked their belief about the cause of his death, they invariably shrugged and stated that it had to be fate.

I ate a late breakfast in a sleek café where automated trays popped out at a touch. I read a collection of Tnpian newspapers. All offered a dedication to Steven Terry, reviewing his accomplishments and what he meant to the Tnpian mind: a symbol of all that was good in the Tnpian civilization. There was no mention of his cause of death, only vague references to "fate."

At one o'clock I was shown into the cluttered office of Loren Hagen. It was fragrant with the smell of the fine tobacco grown in the central area of Tnp; Hagen gripped the holder of a short cigar between yellowing teeth. He motioned to a plump, efficient-looking secretary, and stood up to reach over a desk spread with papers and books to shake my hand with overly enthusiastic eagerness.

I sat down in the chair to which he pointed, as he lowered himself into another behind his desk. "Yes, Mister Forest."

"You knew I was on Tnp?"

"Certainly."

"Then you know why I'm in this office."

"Relates to Steven Terry, of course." He smiled genially as his secretary approached the desk with an old-fashioned silver decanter and two goblets. She poured white liquid into both goblets. I held mine, as Hagen lifted his in toast. "To good will and friendship, Mister Forest," he said. "Volul wine, the best we have here on Tnp."

"Thank you, Mister Hagen." The wine was smooth, sweet, and strong. "Excellent, sir."

"What would you like to know, Mister Forest?"

"You're blunt, Mister Hagen. I'll be the same. Steven Terry is orbiting around up there. Nobody seemingly knows how he died. Why?"

Hagen smiled distantly. "We are a pragmatic culture, Mister Forest. We care what is, not necessarily how it came to be. Mister Terry is dead, as you say. Would knowing how correct the tragedy?"

"It's most unusual, Mister Hagen."

"We like to think of ourselves as an unusual people."

"Is that why Steven Terry's body is constantly monitored by television cameras shown on screens I presume are turned on all over the planet? Is that why people stand in the streets and watch him going overhead with binoculars? Because you are an unusual people?"

"Mister Terry was a hero, sir." He bent his head, studying his littered desk. A small dimple in his right cheek was working rhythmically. "We have been in existence for sixty years, you know that. What is that, in the reckoning of time? Nothing, sir. There are worlds in the galaxy with time virtually imprinted on their history, including Earth. But that is not the case here."

"There was a civilization here before yours."

"A long-ago, nearly forgotten civilization that destroyed itself. Twenty years ago we had a reviving interest in that. Ruins were excavated carefully and with much enthusiasm. Trophies were exhibited. Short histories based on the findings were published. There was a momentary, if feeble, attempt to develop interest in connecting our culture to that one. But it was a negative, Mister Forest. We had no blood ties with it. And how can you identify with a culture that was self-destroyed down to the last man—or woman, if you will? Why buy failure? We didn't, finally. Instead, we have looked to ourselves."

"Blood ties—you're all of Earthian roots."

"Oh, yes. But I think you know how that goes, Mister Forest. We are the near-grown children who have broken the traces with Mother Earth. We have fled the maternal protection as much as possible, and we have, I assure you, no desire to return to that womb. Perhaps in time we shall gain the appreciation of our Earthian heritage. But right now we are much too close to the breakaway. No, Mister Forest, what we Tnpians want is a history of our own, a culture of our own, a feeling that we exist in terms of historic meaning—even if we are but sixty years old."

"And Steven Terry is a part of that historic meaning."

He nodded. "Quite true."

"A twenty-three-year-old boy."

"Judge it in terms of our colony age, sir."

"He became a celebrated figure in your civilization at the age of twelve. Isn't that rather instantaneous?"

128

"Happens, has happened, everywhere, doesn't it?"

"But what precisely did he *do* for Tnp?"

"It wasn't what he did, Mister Forest—not in the sense of what you mean. It was what he represented to us. He represented the chance, the possibility, the dream. It doesn't matter now if he failed to get the opportunity to maneuver the course of our history. It only matters that he was what he was: extraordinarily handsome, mentally superior, physically perfect, an artist, highly skilled in a spacecraft. We settle for what we have, sir. Or had. We had Steven Terry. Now we mourn him. And, I would judge, we shall most assuredly saint him."

"Meantime you have the realistic memorial upon which to mourn and begin the sainting—his body orbiting around this world."

He nodded, smiling gently, watching me with sophisticated eyes.

"I'm wondering about one thing, Mister Hagen. You state quite accurately that he failed to get the opportunity to maneuver the course of your history. Is *that* why he is dead?"

He slid closer to his desk and rested thick forearms against it. His eyes lost any hint of humor. "Go on, Mister Forest."

"First Minister Prinz has held his office for three consecutive terms. He is eligible for one more. Nominating elections are due here in three months. I'm wondering what would have happened if Steven Terry had decided to run for the office of First Minister?"

Hagen's face tightened, shadowing and slitting his eyes. "He would have won the nominating election, as he would have won the general election."

"I understand that you were the original political force behind First Minister Prinz, that you are currently the strongest politico-influence in Tnp."

"You're trying to say something specific, Mister Forest."

"I'm merely conjecturing. Would First Minister Prinz have had a remote chance against young Mister Terry?"

"No."

"He'll have an excellent chance now."

Finally he smiled again. He leaned back. "Very blunt, Mister Forest. Very direct. Very basic. You are implying that perhaps young Terry was murdered in order that First Minister Prinz may win the next election?" He shook his head. "First

Minister Prinz is not running again. It was our plan, our choice, to run Steven Terry in his place. Granted the First Minister had some reservations about Terry's youth. But we felt, finally, that despite it he could carry on the traditions of this government, about which he was in total agreement. We gained nothing by his death, but we lost a very great deal."

"I have only your word on that, sir."

"Check every way you can. You'll find what I've said to be the exact truth."

"How about the opposition? If Steven Terry represented such a certain victory in the next election, wouldn't they have preferred to see him out of the way?"

"Quite probably. But all procedures involved in that final flight Terry made were under absolute government-regulated conditions."

"Still, the procedures might have been infiltrated to create the situation that caused Terry's death."

He nodded again, slowly. "Nevertheless, it has been the *government's* responsibility to investigate the exact cause of death, not the opposition's."

"And that hasn't been done."

He continued to smile at me.

"Why *not*, sir?"

He spread his thick hands. "Somehow, Mister Forest, you must understand us. That is the essential. You must understand us."

The orange light of a fresh day washed into the room I was using at the edge of the landing flat. Benny sat sipping coffee —Earthian coffee that he had cajoled from someone in the commissary.

"Okay, Benny," I said. "The procedure, the equipment, all of it checks out."

"Right, Warden." He removed a check list from his uniform and ran a stubbed thumb down along the points, reciting them. "Aprroved procedure, here. Complete, in my estimation."

"His equipment?"

"He was using prescribed equipment. I've checked duplicates of it. From his flier suit through every component. It

130

was all first-class stuff. There should have been no failure any-where."

"*If* it was in the same condition as the equipment you investigated."

Benny shook his head. "It was checked through three in-spection units, all of them loyal government employees, with perfect records ever since the installation of Prinz into office. And it's a triple-check procedure system. His tank should have been okay. Same with the tube. Helmet was foolproof, as far as I'm concerned. They've developed some fine things here, including that suit and its components. The entire outfit was flawless, one they've used on exploratory shots to the sat-ellites in this system. Where the atmosphere is right, a man can step out of a ship and"—he moved a thumb under his chin in a cutthroat gesture—"deactivate it, just like that. It'll give him complete and sudden freedom. Yet, when it's in use, there's no way it could go wrong."

"What the hell happened to him, Benny?"

Benny shrugged. "One way to find out, Warden."

I nodded, knowing that he was right. The afternoon before, Stoke had flown us around the planet—they were watching that orbiting body everywhere; but we'd found nothing else to solve the puzzle of Terry's death. "Go up and look him over?"

"That's the way."

I thought about it for a time, thinking that the action would complete our role as unwanted intruders. As long as Steven Terry's body was in a light area, cameras and binocu-lars were on him steadily. When we went up there to look him over, it would be under the scrutiny of a large section of the populace, who viewed him as hero and saint. On this planet we would be tampering with something approaching the deep-ly religious. In return, we would receive a proportionate amount of hatred and antagonism.

"When do we go up?" Beeny asked calmly.

"I have something to do first." I carefully tapped out the combination of letters to form the code for Reecie Adams' name.

Her apartment was in the central section of Sovell; the drapes were drawn together, and the interior was softly lighted. She sat gracefully on a couch, wearing a gold robe, suitable for indoor wear, which emphasized the perfection of her figure. Her rich coffee skin was beautiful in that light. Her eyes, so dark that they seemed nearly hidden, were nevertheless watching me with unmistakable disdain. She moved a slim hand over a knee, in an unconscious but ultimately smooth gesture of impatience.

"I'm very sorry if you resent me, Miss Adams," I said quietly. "I'm only here to find out what happened to him. When I do, we'll be gone."

"Leave it alone," she stated in a husky, rich voice.

"I'm afraid we can't. Earth Security Council—"

"What do I care about Earth Security Council? What do I care about anything, now?"

I sat silent, feeling her attraction, yet realizing her deep loss. "How long did you know him, Miss Adams?"

"Seven years," she said flatly.

"How did you meet?"

"I was learning to fly. He was my instructor. We were nothing but children at the time."

"Love at first sight?"

She laughed softly and bitterly. "How could it have been? I was fourteen. He was sixteen. Attraction, I'm sure. You can do that easily enough at that age. But nothing more substantial."

"They mourn him out there, Miss Adams. They feel very deeply about you, too. Because you loved him."

She stood up in a quick cat's movement. *"They!"* She walked with fluid grace to a drape and suddenly drew it open. There were Tnpians down there, I knew, watching the building. The government had supplied two guards at her doorway to prevent unwelcome, if well-meaning, intrusion into her privacy.

"Do you want to tell me about it, Miss Adams?"

"Can't you figure it out, Mister Forest? How it was for him —and then later for me?"

"Perhaps I can now—seeing you in person. But I'd like you to tell me, if you will."

She stalked about the room. "When you are born as good as he was, things come easily and naturally. There is not the

132

great effort to do them. They simply happen for you. I knew that condition too. And what did *they* do?"

"Heroized."

"Heroized, idolized, romanticized! Because why?"

"A new people. There were no other—"

"Exactly! No others before us. So they made him what they wanted him to be! And, later, they did the same to *me!* They had no right!"

"There are no rights in history, Miss Adams. There are simply things that have happened."

"To hell with history!" she said bitingly.

"You can damn it, but you can't change it, once it has happened."

"*They* put him up there! Now let them look, ogle, worship, dream, weep. They are such fools. He was nothing but a *boy!*"

"And you are nothing but a girl?" I asked carefully.

She stopped and stared at me with bright black eyes. "I am a woman, Mister Forest." She laughed, showing white teeth, but there was nothing humorous in that laugh. "Has it not been that way down through all ages? Females my age are never girls, they are always women. But Steven? A twenty-three-year-old boy! *That* is the one they have chosen to saint! It's a mockery!"

"Why did he die, Miss Adams?"

The dark eyes became hidden again. "He simply died. He's there, a corpse. And they want him there, because they never had an honest-to-God martyr before!"

"*Why* is he a martyr? Martyr for *what?*"

"For what they wanted of him! Can't you understand that, Mister Forest? Or do you want me to go down the streets with you and let you see how they look at me?"

"But you can't guess how he died?"

"No!"

"We have to know."

"Why?"

"To retain the balance between planets."

"Something so small, so insignificant, as one boy—"

"It doesn't take much to ruin balances, Miss Adams. We have to know."

"How then will you find out?"

"We'll do something nobody else has seen fit to do, on this planet. We'll go up and inspect his body."

She was breathing quickly. Her eyes had become black fire. "You're going to do that?"

"We're going to do that."

Her voice came out with low, throaty intensity: "Not without me, you're not."

We sat in the circular cabin of the *Wardben,* as Stoke carefully found his position. I looked out the wide window at the white-suited body of Steven Terry moving through space five hundred feet away. I could imagine them down there, watching us, as Stoke maneuvered.

The girl sat opposite me. Benny was directly beside the window, peering at the body intently.

"Closer, Stoke," I said.

The girl was staring at her gloved hands folded across her But don't you see what they'd asked of him? The impossi- by the dead Terry. She would not look out. She would not look at me.

Benny finally nodded. "I'd have to get out there, to make absolutely sure. But I've got it figured now."

I watched the girl now, steadily; I saw her lids flicker. "How, Benny?"

"He deactivated the suit. He's a suicide."

The girl drew in her breath. She looked at me with fright and pain showing in the dark depths of her eyes.

"I'll put on a thruster and go out to verify," I said softly.

Her head moved from side to side. "That last night we were together—he wanted me to marry him. Right away. They'd asked him to run for the office of First Minister. He was frightened. Can you believe that? Steven Terry frightened? But don't you see what they'd asked of him? The impossible! And he'd known it!"

"Go on, Reecie," I said gently.

"He needed me, as his wife. But I couldn't. I simply *couldn't!*"

"Why not?"

"I didn't love him! He was only a child. Don't you understand? He was brought up for the first part of his life in that home of *machines!* No matter his intellect, no matter his

skills, no matter anything, he was underdeveloped in that
emotional area he wanted to share with me. How can a child
love any way other than he might a parent? I wasn't his
parent. I was a *woman*, Mister Forest! In time—yes; it might
have worked. When his emotional development reached
everything else he'd accomplished, then, yes. I might have
loved him properly in return. But not *that* night. It was the
first defeat for him in his entire life! Please understand, Mister
Forest! He tried to be everything they wanted him to be, but
he wasn't truly. Underneath all, he was a frightened boy. I
couldn't . . ."

I looked out at that orbiting statue. They had wanted something of him, all right, and it had been merely everything.
He'd known he couldn't give it to them, if he'd gone on living.
And this way, orbiting in this fashion, a space-lofted monu-
ment to the hopes, desires, dreams, to all that they wanted, he
had not let them down. One defeat, created by this girl's natural failure to love him back as he'd hoped she could, had
shaken the foundation of everything he'd hoped to represent
to his people. It had been enough to make him create that
final self-destructive act . . .

She was looking out there, too. Her eyes were still wide and
frightened and wholly hurt. "He *couldn't* have," she whispered. "It must have been something else. Fate, God, the
gods . . ."

"I'm going out there, Reecie, to make sure."

She shook her head quickly. "Don't, please. We don't *want*
to know. I told First Minister Prinz what had happened that
last night. Maybe he thought of it this way all along. That's
why there was no investigation. Don't you understand, Mister
Forest? Suicide? They *can't* know that. It would ruin the
legend!"

"We have to know."

"*I'll* go out then. Let me use your thruster. Please, Mister
Forest. If I know positively that he . . ."

"It's my job."

"But they're watching! It won't be right for you. They'll accept me. Please. Let me be the one to know for sure!"

I was silent for an interval. Finally I nodded.

Benny and I watched her swing skillfully through space in her white suit. There was something dreamlike about her movement, and I could understand how they would feel down there, watching the screens, staring through their binoculars.

She glided nearer to him, then her delicate, gloved hands were reaching out. Her face-window touched his. She knew now, I thought . . .

I saw the movement of her right hand, hidden from the thousands upon thousands watching below. She made a cut-throat motion directly beneath her chin.

"My God!" I sat frozen for a few seconds, then I jumped up. But Benny said:

"No good, Warden. No time. She's . . ."

I forced myself to look again. She'd moved his arms so that they were around her. And hers were around him. They were in orbit in that embrace.

I moved to the visio-radio. "First Minister Prinz, Stoke."

Moments later Stoke nodded. "Okay, Warden."

I looked at the image forming on the screen. The flat-silver eyes of Prinz stared back at me.

"She's dead," I said wearily.

"How?"

"I don't know. She wanted to go out, to see him again. I'd judge . . . heartbreak."

He nodded slowly. "Fate."

"Act of God . . . the gods."

"Thank you, Mister Forest."

I nodded, knowing that our work was done here now. "Good-bye, sir."

To the
Dark Star

by Robert Silverberg

We came to the dark star, the microcephalon and the
adapted girl and I, and our struggle began. A poorly assorted
lot we were, to begin with. The microcephalon hailed from
Quendar IV, where they grow their people with greasy gray
skins, looming shoulders, and virtually no heads at all. He—it
—was wholly alien, at least. The girl was not, and so I hated
her.

She came from a world in the Procyon system, where the
air was more or less Earth-type, but the gravity was double
ours. There were other differences, too. She was thick through
the shoulders, thick through the waist, a block of flesh. The
genetic surgeons had begun with human raw material, but
they had transformed it into something nearly as alien as the
microcephalon. Nearly.

We were a scientific team, so they said. Sent out to observe
the last moments of a dying star. A great interstellar effort.
Pick three specialists at random, put them in a ship, hurl them
halfway across the universe to observe what man had never
observed before. A fine idea. Noble. Inspiring. We knew our
subject well. We were ideal.

But we felt no urge to cooperate, because we hated one another.

The adapted girl—Miranda—was at the controls the day that the dark star actually came into sight. She spent hours studying it before she deigned to let us know that we were at our destination. Then she buzzed us out of our quarters.

I entered the scanning room. Miranda's muscular bulk overflowed the glossy chair before the main screen. The microcephalon stood beside her, a squat figure on a tripodlike arrangement of bony legs, the great shoulders hunched and virtually concealed the tiny cupola of the head. There was no real reason why an organism's brain *had* to be in its skull, and not safely tucked away in the thorax; but I had never grown accustomed to the sight of the creature. I fear I have little tolerance for aliens.

"Look," Miranda said, and the screen glowed.

The dark star hung in dead center, at a distance of perhaps eight light-days—as close as we dared to come. It was not quite dead, and not quite dark. I stared in awe. It was a huge thing, some four solar masses, the imposing remnant of a gigantic star. On the screen there glowed what looked like an enormous lava field. Islands of ash and slag the size of worlds drifted in a sea of molten and glowing magma. A dull red illumination burnished the screen. Black against crimson, the ruined star still throbbed with ancient power. In the depths of that monstrous slag heap, compressed nuclei groaned and gasped. Once the radiance of this star had lit a solar system; but I did not dare think of the billions of years that had passed since then, nor of the possible civilizations that had hailed the source of all light and warmth before the catastrophe.

Miranda said, "I've picked up the thermals already. The surface temperature averages about nine hundred degrees. There's no chance of the landing."

I scowled at her. "What good is the *average* temperature? Get a specific. One of those islands—"

"The ash masses are radiating at two hundred and fifty degrees. The interstices go from one thousand degrees on up. Everything works out to a mean of nine hundred degrees, and you'd melt in an instant if you went down there. You're welcome to go, brother. With my blessing."

"I didn't say—"

"You implied that there'd be a safe place to land on that fireball," Miranda snapped. Her voice was a basso boom; there was plenty of resonance space in that vast chest of hers. "You snidely cast doubt on my ability to—"

"We will use the crawler to make our inspection," said the microcephalon in its reasonable way. "There never was any plan to make a physical landing on the star."

Miranda subsided. I stared in awe at the sight that filled our screen.

A star takes a long time to die, and the relict I viewed impressed me with its colossal age. It had blazed for billions of years, until the hydrogen that was its fuel had at last been exhausted, and its thermonuclear furnace started to sputter and go out. A star has defenses against growing cold; as its fuel supply dwindles, it begins to contract, raising its density and converting gravitational potential energy into thermal energy. It takes on new life; now a white dwarf, with a density of tons per cubic inch, it burns in a stable way until at last it grows dark.

We have studied white dwarfs for centuries, and we know their secrets—so we think. A cup of matter from a white dwarf now orbits the observatory on Pluto for our further illumination.

But the star of our screen was different.

It had once been a large star—greater than the Chandrasekhar limit, 1.2 solar masses. Thus it was not content to shrink step by step to the status of a white dwarf. The stellar core grew so dense that catastrophe came before stability; when it had converted all its hydrogen to iron-56, it fell into catastrophic collapse and went supernova. A shock wave ran through the core, converting the kinetic energy of collapse into heat. Neutrinos spewed outward; the envelope of the star reached temperatures upwards of two hundred billion degrees; thermal energy became intense radiation, streaming away from the agonized star and shedding the luminosity of a galaxy for a brief, fitful moment.

What we beheld now was the core left behind by the supernova explosion. Even after that awesome fury, what was intact was of great mass. The shattered hulk had been cooling for eons, cooling toward the final death. For a small star, that death would be the simple death of coldness: the ultimate burnout, the black dwarf drifting through the void like a hideous mound of ash, lightless, without warmth. But this our stellar core was still beyond the Chandrasekhar limit. A special death was reserved for it, a weird and improbable death.

And that was why we had come to watch it perish, the microcephalon and the adapted girl and I.

I parked our small vessel in an orbit that gave the dark star plenty of room. Miranda busied herself with her measurements and computations. The microcephalon had more abstruse things to do. The work was well divided; we each had our chores. The expense of sending a ship so great a distance had necessarily limited the size of the expedition. Three of us: a representative of the basic human stock, a representative of the adapted colonists, a representative of the race of microcephalons, the Quendar people, the only other intelligent beings in the known universe.

Three dedicated scientists. And, therefore, three who would live in serene harmony during the course of the work, since as everyone knows scientists have no emotions and think only of their professional mysteries. As everyone knows. When did that myth start to circulate, anyway?

I said to Miranda, "Where are the figures for radial oscillation?"

She replied, "See my report. It'll be published early next year in—"

"Damn you, are you doing that deliberately? I need those figures now!"

"Give me your totals on the mass-density curve, then."

"They aren't ready. All I've got is raw data."

"That's a lie! The computer's been running for days! I've seen it," she boomed at me.

I was ready to leap at her throat. It would have been a mighty battle; her three-hundred-pound body was not trained for personal combat, as mine was, but she had all the advantages of strength and size. Could I club her in some vital place before she broke me in half? I weighed my options.

Then the microcephalon appeared and made peace once more, with a few feather-soft words.

Only the alien among us seemed to conform at all to the stereotype of that emotionless abstraction, "the scientist." It was not true, of course; for all we could tell, the microcephalon seethed with jealousies and lusts and angers, but we had no clue to their outward manifestation. Its voice was as flat as a vocoder transmission. The creature moved peacefully among us, the mediator between Miranda and me. I despised it for its mask of tranquility. I suspected, too, that the microcephalon loathed the two of us for our willingness to vent our emotions, and took a sadistic pleasure from asserting superiority by calming us.

We returned to our research. We still had some time before the last collapse of the dark star.

It had cooled nearly to death. Now there was still some thermonuclear activity within that bizarre core, enough to keep the star too warm for an actual landing. It was radiating primarily in the optical band of the spectrum, and by stellar standards its temperature was nil, but for us it would be like prowling the heart of a live volcano.

Finding the star had been a chore. Its luminosity was so low that it could not be detected optically at a greater distance than a light-month or so; it had been spotted by a satellite-born X-ray telescope that had detected the emanations of the degenerate neutron gas of the core. Now we gathered around and performed our functions of measurement. We recorded things like neutron drip and electron capture. We computed the time remaining before the final collapse. Where necessary, we collaborated; most of the time we went our separate ways. The tension aboard ship was nasty. Miranda went out of her way to provoke me. And, though I like to think that I was beyond and above her beastliness, I have to confess that I matched her, obstruction for obstruction. Our alien companion never made any overt attempt to annoy us; but indirect aggression can be maddening in close quarters, and the microcephalon's benign indifference to us was as potent a force for dissonance as Miranda's outright shrewishness or my own deliberately mulish responses.

The star hung in our viewscreen, bubbling with vitality that belied its dying state. The islands of slag, thousands of miles in diameter, broke free and drifted at random on the sea of inner flame. Now and then spouting eruptions of stripped particles came heaving up out of the core. Our figures showed that the final collapse was drawing near, and that meant that an awkward choice was upon us. Someone was going to have to monitor the last moments of the dark star. The risks were high. It could be fatal.

None of us mentioned that ultimate responsibility.

We moved toward the climax of our work. Miranda continued to annoy me in every way, sheerly for the devilishness of it. How I hated her! We had begun this voyage coolly, with nothing dividing us but professional jealousy. But the months of proximity had turned our quarrel into a personal feud. The mere sight of her maddened me, and I'm sure she reacted the same way. She devoted her energies to an immature attempt to trouble me. Lately she took to walking around the ship in the nude, I suspect trying to stir some spark of sexual feeling in me that she could douse with a blunt, mocking refusal. The trouble was that I could feel no desire whatever for a grotesque adapted creature like Miranda, a mound of muscle and bone twice my size. The sight of her massive udders and monumental buttocks stirred nothing in me but disgust.

The witch! Was it desire she was trying to kindle by exposing herself that way, or loathing? Either way, she had me. She must have known that.

In our third month in orbit around the dark star, the microcephalon announced, "The coordinates show an approach to the Schwarzschild radius. It is time to send our vehicle to the surface of the star."

"Which one of us rides monitor?" I asked.

Miranda's beefy hand shot out at me. "You do."

"I think you're better equipped to make the observations," I told her sweetly.

"Thank you, no."

"We must draw lots," said the microcephalon.

"Unfair," said Miranda. She glared at me. "He'll do something to rig the odds. I couldn't trust him."

"How else can we choose?" the alien asked.

"We can vote," I suggested. "I nominate Miranda."

"I nominate him," she snapped.

The microcephalon put his ropy tentacles across the tiny nodule of skull between his shoulders. "Since I did not choose to nominate myself," he said mildly, "it falls to me to make a deciding choice between the two of you. I refuse the responsibility. Another method must be found."

142

We let the matter drop for the moment. We still had a few more days before the critical time was at hand.

With all my heart I wished Miranda into the monitor capsule. It would mean at best her death, at worst a sober muting of her abrasive personality, if she were the one who sat in vicariously on the throes of the dark star. I was willing to stop at nothing to give her that remarkable and demolishing experience.

What was going to happen to our star may sound strange to a layman, but the theory had been outlined by Einstein and Schwarzschild a thousand years ago, and had been confirmed many times, though never until our expedition had it been observed at close range. When matter reaches a sufficiently high density, it can force the local curvature of space to close around itself, forming a pocket isolated from the rest of the universe. A collapsing supernova core creates just such a Schwarzschild singularity. After it has cooled to near-zero temperature, a core of the proper Chandrasekhar mass undergoes a violent collapse to zero volume, simultaneously attaining an infinite density.

In a way, it swallows itself and vanishes from this universe —for how could the fabric of the continuum tolerate a point of infinite density and zero volume?

Such collapses are rare. Most stars come to a state of cold equilibrium and remain there. We were on the threshold of a singularity, and we were in a position to put an observer vehicle right on the surface of the cold star, sending back an exact description of the events up until the final moment when the collapsing core broke through the walls of the universe and disappeared.

Someone had to ride gain on the equipment, though. Which meant, in effect, vicariously participating in the death of the star. We had learned in other cases that it becomes difficult for the monitor to distinguish between reality and effect; he accepts the sensory percepts from the distant pickup as his own experience. A kind of psychic backlash results; often, an unwary brain is burned out entirely.

What impact would the direct experience of being crushed out of existence in a singularity have on a monitoring observer?

I was eager to find out. But not with myself as the sacrificial victim.

I cast about for some way to get Miranda into that capsule. She, of course, was doing the same for me. It was she who made the first move by attempting to drug me into compliance.

What drug she used, I have no idea. Her people are fond of the non-addictive hallucinogens, which help them break the monotony of their stark oversized world. Somehow Miranda interfered with the programming of my food supply and introduced one of her pet alkaloids. I began to feel the effects an hour after I had eaten. I walked to the screen to study the surging mass of the dark star—much changed from its appearance of only a few months before—and as I looked, the image on the screen began to swirl and melt, and tongues of flame did an eerie dance along the horizons of the star.

I clung to the rail. Sweat broke from my pores. Was the ship liquefying? The floor heaved and bucked beneath me. I looked at the back of my hand and saw continents of ash set in a grouting of fiery magma.

Miranda stood behind me. "Come with me to the capsule," she murmured. "The monitor's ready for launching now. You'll find it wonderful to see the last moments."

Lurching after her, I padded through the strangely altered ship. Miranda's adapted form was even more alien than usual; her musculature rippled and flowed, her golden hair held all the colors of the spectrum, her flesh was oddly puckered and cratered, with wiry filaments emerging from the skin. I felt quite calm about entering the capsule. She slid back the hatch, revealing the gleaming console of the panel within, and I began to enter, and then suddenly the hallucination deepened and I saw in the darkness of the capsule a devil beyond all imagination.

I dropped to the floor and lay there twitching.

Miranda seized me. To her I was no more than a doll. She lifted me, began to thrust me into the capsule. Perspiration soaked me. Reality returned. I slipped from her grasp and wriggled away, rolling toward the bulkhead. Like a beast of primordial forests she came ponderously after me.

"No," I said. "I won't go."

She halted. Her face twisted in anger, and she turned away

from me in defeat. I lay panting and quivering until my mind was purged of phantoms. It had been close.

It was my turn a short while later. Fight force with force, I told myself. I could not risk more of Miranda's treachery. Time was running short.

From our surgical kit I took a hypnoprobe used for anesthesia, and rigged it in series with one of Miranda's telescope antennae. Programming it for induction of docility, I left it to go to work on her. When she made her observations, the hypnoprobe would purr its siren song of sinister coaxing, and—perhaps—Miranda would bend to my wishes.

It did not work.

I watched her going to her telescopes. I saw her broad-beamed form settling in place. In my mind I heard the hypnoprobe's gentle whisper as I knew it must sound to Miranda. It was telling her to relax, to obey. "The capsule . . . get into the capsule . . . you will monitor the crawler . . . you . . . you . . . you will do it. . . ."

I waited for her to arise and move like a sleepwalker to the waiting capsule. Her tawny body was motionless. Muscles rippled beneath that obscenely bare flesh. The probe had her! Yes! It was getting to her!

No.

She clawed at the telescope as though it were a steel-tipped wasp drilling for her brain. The barrel recoiled, and she pushed herself away from it, whirling around. Her eyes glowed with rage. Her enormous body reared up before me. She seemed half berserk. The probe had had some effect on her; I could see her dizzied strides, and knew that she was awry. But it had not been potent enough. Something within that adapted brain of hers gave her the strength to fight off the murky shroud of hypnotism.

"You did that!" she roared. "You gimmicked the telescope, didn't you?"

"I don't know what you mean, Miranda."

"Liar! Fraud! Sneak!"

"Calm down. You're rocking us out of orbit."

"I'll rock all I want! What was that thing that had its fingers in my brain? You put it there! What was it, the hypnoprobe you used?"

"Yes," I admitted coolly. "And what was it you put into my food? Which hallucinogen?"

"It didn't work."

"Neither did my hypnoprobe. Miranda, someone's got to get into that capsule. In a few hours we'll be at the critical point. We don't dare come back without the essential observations. Make the sacrifice."

"For *you?*"

"For science," I said, appealing to that noble abstraction.

I got the horselaugh I deserved. Then Miranda strode toward me. She had recovered her coordination in full, now, and it seemed as though she were planning to thrust me into the capsule by main force. Her ponderous arms enfolded me. The stink of her thickened hide made me retch. I felt ribs creaking within me. I hammered at her body, searching for the pressure points that would drop her in a felled heap. We punished each other cruelly, grunting back and forth across the cabin. It was a fierce contest of skill against mass. She would not fall, and I would not crush.

The toneless buzz of the microcephalon said, "Release each other. The collapsing star is nearing its Schwarzschild radius. We must act now."

Miranda's arms slipped away from me. I stepped back, glowering at her, to suck breath into my battered body. Livid bruises were appearing on her skin. We had come to a mutual awareness of mutual strength; but the capsule still was empty. Hatred hovered like a globe of ball lightning between us. The gray, greasy alien creature stood to one side.

I would not care to guess which of us had the idea first, Miranda or I. But we moved swiftly. The microcephalon scarcely murmured a word of protest as we hustled it down the passage and into the room that held the capsule. Miranda was smiling. I felt relief. She held the alien tight while I opened the hatch, and then she thrust it through. We dogged the hatch together.

"Launch the crawler," she said.

I nodded and went to the controls. Like a dart from a blowgun the crawler housing was expelled from our ship and journeyed under high acceleration to the surface of the dark star. It contained a compact vehicle with sturdy jointed legs, controlled by remote pickup from the observation capsule aboard ship. As the observer moved arms and feet within the control harnesses, servo relays actuated the hydraulic pistons in the crawler, eight light-days away. It moved in parallel response, clambering over the slag heaps of a solar surface that no organic life could endure.

The microcephalon operated the crawler with skill. We watched through the shielded video pickups, getting a close-range view of that inferno. Even a cold sun is more terrifyingly hot than any planet of man.

The signals coming from the star altered with each moment, as the full force of the red-shift gripped the fading light. Something unutterably strange was taking place down there; and the mind of our microcephalon was rooted to the scene. Tidal gravitational forces lashed the star. The crawler was lifted, heaved, compressed, subjected to strains that slowly ripped it apart. The alien witnessed it all, and dictated an account of what he saw, slowly, methodically, without a flicker of fear.

The singularity approached. The tidal forces aspired toward infinity. The microcephalon sounded bewildered at last as it attempted to describe the topological phenomena that no eye had seen before. Infinite density, zero volume—how did the mind comprehend it? The crawler was contorted into an inconceivable shape; and yet its sensors obstinately continued to relay data, filtered through the mind of the microcephalon and into our computer banks.

Then came silence. Our screens went dead. The unthinkable had at last occurred, and the dark star had passed within the radius of singularity. It had collapsed into oblivion, taking with it the crawler. To the alien in the observation capsule aboard our ship, it was as though he too had vanished into that pocket of hyperspace that passed all understanding.

I looked toward the heavens. The dark star was gone. Our detectors picked up the outpouring of energy that marked its annihilation. We were buffeted briefly on the wave of force that ripped outward from the place where the star had been, and then all was calm.

Miranda and I exchanged glances.

"Let the microcephalon out," I said.

She opened the hatch. The alien sat quite calmly at the con-

147

trol console. It did not speak. Miranda assisted it from the capsule. Its eyes were expressionless; but they had never shown anything, anyway.

We are on our way back to the worlds of our galaxy, now. The mission has been accomplished. We have relayed priceless and unique data.

The microcephalon has not spoken since we removed it from the capsule. I do not believe it will speak again.

Miranda and I perform our chores in harmony. The hostility between us is gone. We are partners in crime, now; edgy with guilt that we do not admit to one another. We tend our shipmate with loving care.

Someone had to make the obervations, after all. There were no volunteers. The situation called for force, or the deadlock would never have been broken.

But Miranda and I hated each other, you say? Why, then, should we cooperate?

We both are humans, Miranda and I. The microcephalon is not. In the end, that made the difference. In the last analysis, Miranda and I decided that we humans must stick together. There are ties that bind.

We speed onward toward civilization.

She smiles at me. I do not find her hateful now. The microcephalon is silent.

A Night in Elf Hill

#################################### **by Norman Spinrad**

Dear Fred:

Yeah, it's your brother Spence after all these years, and of course I'm yelling for help. Just spare me the I-told-you-sos and the psychiatrist's pounce. So I'm a black sheep and a miscreant and a neurotic personality. We never could quite stand each other even when we were kids, and when you became a shrink and I Shipped Out, that really tore it. The reality of inner space versus the escapism of outer space, maturity versus perpetual adolescence, isn't that what you said? Sometimes I think you were born speaking that jargon, and if you'll pardon my saying so, I still think it's horse-hockey.

But the bitch is that now I find myself urgently in need of your brand of horse-hockey. I've got something I've got to tell to somebody, something that's been eating me up for a year, something way over my head. Something you only tell a brother or a shrink—and for all your squareness, Fred, at least you're both.

I suppose I've got you good and confused by now, just like in the bad old days, but I hope I've got you as intrigued as bugged.

Don't go putting things in my mouth, though; I've got no

regrets. Seventeen years in space, and I don't regret a minute of it. But you never could understand that. Remember? I'd tell you about the kick of ten new planets every year, of a new woman on every one of 'em, of the greener grass just beyond the planet beyond the next one, and what I'd get from you is long lectures on "flight from reality" and "compulsive satyrism." The only reason I'm raking up these tired old coals, *Herr Doktor,* is that it all bears on the problem that I'm going to do my damnedest to try and dump in your lap.

Yeah, space is my oyster, always has been, always will be—and that's my only regret. The knowledge that eighteen years of it is all I can ever have.

You know how the time limit on Merchant Service Papers works, or at least you should, since shrinks like you stuck us with the system. When you apply for Papers, they give you a solid week of physical and mental examinations, everything in the book and some things that aren't, and they tell you just how long they figure you can stand the jumping in and out of subspace, the accelerations, the pressures, the tensions. They tell you how long, and they put it down on your Papers. This man is certified for eighteen years in space and not a millisecond longer. The moving finger writes, and all that. . . . Actually, I've got no fair reason to complain: eighteen years is Good Time. The average is closer to fifteen.

It's a nice safe system. No one suddenly goes ape and wrecks a ship, like in the bad old days. No spacer, shipping far beyond his endurance, comes home a shattered hulk from Farside Syndrome anymore.

Yeah, a good, safe, secure system. The only thing wrong with it is that you know you have that date hanging over your head, and you know that under the rules the day will come when you start collecting that Mustering Out Pension (a nice piece of change every year as long as you live—even to a high-priced shrink like you, Fred), and get that last free ride to the planet of your choice.

Sure, you think it's a sweet set-up. *You* would. Eighteen years of your life in return for financial security in perpetuity. Why don't you go to Port Kennedy and take a good hard look at all those old men sitting in the sun, living off their nice fat pensions and watching the ships taking off for the stars like one-eyed cats peeping in a seafood store? Old men of thirty-five or forty. Ask *them* if it's such a sweet set-up! How would you like to be put out to pasture when you're forty? After eighteen years, what do you have to live for but the next planet? That last free ride back to Earth is the sickest joke there is. It's not for me. In the bad old days, they let you ship out till it killed you, and ask any of the hulks that haunt Port Kennedy if that wasn't the more merciful way.

Man, I'm sure glad this is a letter, because I can all but hear you bellowing "I told you so." What was it you used to call Shipping Out, "A night in Elf Hill"? Where a man goes into the hall of the elves for one night of partying, and the next day, when he comes out, a hundred years have passed, and he's an old, old man and his life is over. . . . I can hear you telling me that I can't find myself by searching the galaxy, that I've got to look within, and now look at you, Spence, you're a hollow shell, a thirty-eight-year-old adolescent. I can see you shaking your head with infinite sadness and infinite wisdom, and you should be glad this isn't face-to-face too, 'cause I'd kick your sanctimonious teeth down your throat, and you know that I always could lick you.

Suffice it to say that unless you can come up with some pearl of wisdom from out of your bottomless pit of middle-aged maturity, and don't get me wrong, Fred, I hope to God you can, when I'm Mustered Out next year, that last trip won't be back to Earth. It'll be to Mindalla.

I know, I know, you never heard of Mindalla. Who has? It's a nothing little planet orbiting a G-4 sun. Colonized about a century ago. Maybe fifteen million yokums living off a piddling mining industry on one continent. That's Mindalla. Ten thousand mudballs just like it scattered all over the galaxy. But I'm afraid, really afraid, that unless you can stop me, I'm going back. Going back to stay.

I made my first planetfall on Mindalla a little over a year ago, on a freighter from Sidewinder, carrying the kind of cargo we just don't talk about. Fortunately, it's a big, big galaxy, and there are so many planets in it that you never have to go back to a single one, even if your Papers go all the way to the twenty-year maximum.

And so, I believed at the time, this would be my first and last visit to Mindalla. I mean, when you've been in space as

long as I have, seen hundreds of cities on hundreds of planets
—G'dana, Hespa, the Ruby Beach of Modow, the whole wild
lot—Mindalla is strictly nowheresville.

The population is small, there's only one town with nerve
enough to call itself a city, the outback has been pretty
thoroughly explored by air, no interesting local beasties, no
natives. And the colony is just not old enough to have really
marinated, if you dig, become decadent enough to appeal to
my peculiar tastes. . . . But let's not get into *that*.

Still, like it or not, I had three days on this mudball, and I
knew from long experience that a planet's just too big a place
to be a total nonentity. That's why I went into space in the
first place; that's where it's really at. Not all that crap about
"the vast spaces between the stars." Space itself is creation's
most total bore. What makes a man Ship Out is just being a
kid on Earth, and looking up at all those stars, and knowing
that they all own whole worlds, and that each of 'em *is* a
world, as full of surprises as Earth was when Adam and his
chick got themselves booted out of Eden. I guess that's it—
you've got to dig surprises. Man like me *hates* security as
much as you love it.

So I knew there had to be *something* for me on Mindalla, a
new taste, a new sound, a new woman. A nice surprise. . . .

Well, I wandered from bar to bar, my usual S.O.P., and to
make a long, tedious story short, I came up with only two little goodies, and one of 'em seemed to be just a fairy story at
first.

But the second concerned the Race With No Name. The
Race had left one of its weird ruins on Mindalla.

Even *you* must know about the Race With No Name. Billions of years ago, before Man was even a far-distant gleam in
some dinosaur's eye, before the 'Bodas or the Dreers, or any
of the other races that are around today ever existed, the Race
With No Name owned this galaxy, from the Center clear to
the Magellanic Clouds. A billion years ago, they disappeared,
died out, or migrated elsewhere, or God-knows-what, leaving
nothing but ruins on thousands of planets. If you can call
lumps of some metal that assay out stainless steel but hasn't
rusted at all in a billion years ruins. A lump of the stuff here,
a whole mountain of it there, weathered to dust by a billion
years of time and wind, twenty or so artifacts that no one un-

derstands, scattered throughout the known galaxy—the Race With No Name.

But you know that. What you don't know is what the Race means to spacers. It's our own private little nightmare that somewhere, somehow, some of 'em are still around, and that one day we're going to run into them, in subspace, or on some forgotten planet on the Rim. . . . A race a billion years gone, a race that was young when the galaxy was coalescing, a race that had as much in common with us as we do with worms . . . A race that we can't be sure doesn't still exist, somewhere . . .

And the Race With No Name left a few lumps of metal on Mindalla, as they did on thousands of other planets. Nothing unusual . . . But then there was that local fairy story. . . .

It seems that a few decades ago, a Mindallan who had been a spacer settled down on his pension near something called the Great Swamp. Apparently, he wigged out—was known to rave about someplace in the Swamp that was the "most beautiful city in the galaxy." Of course, there was no such thing in the Swamp. And one day, he just disappeared and they never found his body. The locals claimed that other men had disappeared into the Great Swamp, but nobody I talked to could name names.

Just the usual crock, eh? But the Race With No Name had left a ruin on Mindalla, and when you added that to the fairy story, you came up with something that smelled of artifact.

I guess they've found maybe two dozen intact artifacts of the Race With No Name. I lose count. There's the Solid Hole on Beauchamp, the Time Trap on Flor del Cielo, the Subspace Block on Misty, that horrible thing they haven't even named on Channing, the thing that turns living creatures inside out. . . . No one knows what any of the damned things really are, and I suppose we never will. Maybe I *hope* we never will.

But I got the smell of artifact on Mindalla. Somewhere in that swamp was . . . *something*. No matter how many men have died, or worse, because of them, I still never heard of a spacer who could resist the lure of discovering an artifact. Don't ask me why. Why do people pick at scabs, *Herr Doktor?*

So I rented a flitter, bought some tinned food, leased an

energy-rifle which everyone assured me was about as necessary as a Conversion Bomb, and set out for the Great Swamp.

The Swamp was where it was supposed to be—about four hundred miles east of the city. "Great Swamp" turned out to be local hyperbole, of course—you could lose it in the Everglades.

I set the flitter down in a clearing near the center of the Swamp. The clearing was ringed with trees—something between palms and mangroves; gnarled, ringed trunks, big, bright-green, feathery leaves. The ground was coal-black, the way it sometimes is around a volcano on Earth, only here it was soggy, half-mud, interlaced with hundreds of sluggish little streams. In short, a swamp.

I put a small radio direction finder in my pocket, turned on the flitter's beacon, hoisted my small pack, slung the energy-rifle over my shoulder, and set off rather noisily to get the lay of the land.

One weird thing—the trees were lousy with a kind of feathery stuff like Spanish moss, long globs of it hanging everywhere. It was a deep, deep red, and it gave you the feeling that you were walking through perpetual sunset. Kind of eerie, maybe, but also sort of soothing.

Quite a few critters around—ugly littly lumpy fish like mudpuppies in the streams, small six-legged blue lizards all over the place, octopoid things swinging in the trees by their tentacles like monkeys—but nothing big enough to worry about, even without the rifle.

Actually, I suppose you'd go for the place—you always were a nature nut, and this swamp had what you'd call atmosphere, what with that red moss all over everything and the black soil, and those octopoids in the trees, covered with a golden fuzz and gabbling like turkeys. Now you know me, Fred, I'm strictly a city boy, my idea of beauty is Greater New York, or Bay City, or Riallo. But I must admit that I sort of dug the place. It put me at ease, it even smelled kind of sweet and musky, as I went deeper into it.

And, of course, that's when I should've started to sweat. I don't care how tame a planet is, it just shouldn't *seem* harmless if it isn't Earth. Every planet is different from every other in thousands of ways, and at least *one* of those differences should be the kind that makes a man look behind him. Besides, every other extraterrestrial swamp I've ever seen stank like an open cesspool.

Well, I must've just wandered around for hours before I felt . . . how can I describe it? A kind of scratchy shiver in my head, like running a broken fingernail down a piece of slate. An awful feeling, but it just came and went in a moment, and all of a sudden, things got kind of dreamylike.

The moss seemed to get thicker, the light richer, heavier. And all of a sudden, the air was full of tiny, neon-colored birds, no bigger than beetles, like a whole aquarium full of flying tropical fish, and they almost seemed to be whistling in harmony.

I went on in a kind of daze, and that scratchy feeling came and went again, and a very funny thing happened. I found myself remembering all kinds of things: women I had known, the taste of Blandi wine and fried prawns, the smell of Shondor aphrofume, the sun flashing on the Ruby Beach, the carnival feel of Riallo. . . . Good things, a whole lifeful of good things, all whipping through my mind like someone had recorded the best moments of my life on tape and was playing the whole tape back, a hundred times normal speed.

It was like being high on mescal and bhang and duprish all at once, and I got flashes of *that* too, I mean memories of what being high was really like, mixed in with the rest of it.

I forgot everything—the reason I was in the Swamp, the fact that I had to be back on the ship in two days, even my depression at my impending Mustering Out. I just wandered around reliving the best moments of my life at breakneck speed.

And then I felt that awful, nerve-tingling feeling again, stronger this time. It seemed to last for hours, and then it was gone again, and . . .

I was standing on top of a little hill. And there below me, where it just couldn't possibly be, was a city. *The* city. The city the Mindallan spacer had raved about. And he had been dead right. It *was* the most beautiful place in the galaxy.

I've seen a thousand cities on hundreds of planets. I've seen Riallo on Topaz which makes Greater New York look like a dirty little milltown. Fred, this place made Riallo look like a cluster of mud huts.

Translucent towers of emerald a mile high, piercing the clouds like artificial mountains, hundreds of them, and the streets of the city wound around their feet, streets jammed with buildings from a hundred planets and cultures—Argolian force-pavilions, mosques, Boharaanan fhars, skyscrapers, stadia, ziggurats—all shimmering and flickering in the everchanging light that seemed to come from the towers, that made the sky above the city a great rainbow aurora.

A river separated the foot of my hill from the city. A bridge crossed the river, and a road crossed the bridge. The road was a ribbon of burnished silver. The bridge was a single, arching, dazzling living crystal that might've been diamond. The river was a flow of liquid gold.

The capital city of the universe. Utterly stupefying, utterly impossible . . . and yet, I had that, what do you call it, *déjà vu* feeling that I had somehow seen it before.

What can I say, Fred? I must've been out of my head. It couldn't be there, but it was, and I couldn't even think of all the impossibilities of the situation, the sheer insanity of it all. I ran down that hill like a sex-starved hermit toward a Mexican border town, down the silver road, across the diamond bridge, and I was *there*, totally *there*.

Ever been in Rio at the height of Carnival? Ever spent Mardi Gras in Old New Orleans? Ever heard of how Riallo becomes one great citywide party on Settling Day Eve? Well, triple that. Raise it to its own power, take a big drag of opium, and, man, you won't even come close.

It just sucked me in—*whoosh*. The streets were simply boiling with people and beings. Golden Women from Topaz, tall green Jungle Masters from Mizzan, Steppenvolke from Siegfried dressed in clinging mirror-suits, lemur-faced Cheeringbodas, women with their hair piled into nests for shimmering Grellan Glass Butterflies . . . Beings from a thousand planets, all babbling, laughing. . . . Carnival sounds: laughter, singing, music. Carnival smells: perfume, frying food, hashish smoke, wine, women.

I felt as if I had stepped into the Arabian Nights. Any minute a flying carpet might float by. I felt as if I had been searching for this place, this huge Carnival, this moment in time, all my life. I wanted to laugh and scream and cry.

And then I felt that itching in my mind again, and I saw

her coming toward me, straight toward me through that packed throng, which seemed to drift away before her like fog melting away in the sun.

She was wearing those now-opaque, now-transparent golden robes from Topaz. She was almost my height, had exotic oriental features but bone-white skin. Luminous emerald hair cascaded onto her shoulders. She had a slim-but-full body, and through a momentary transparency in her robes, I saw that her nipples were an impossible blood-red, matching the color of her small, full lips.

She was like no woman anyone had ever seen, and yet as she stood before me, I had that uncanny *déjà vu* feeling again. I knew her, but from where? Ridiculous. How could any man forget a woman like *this*?

She touched my hand, and a thrill went through me like a jolt from a Pleasurebox. *"Hello,"* she said, and the sound of her voice turned my knees to jello. "I've been waiting for you. We've all been waiting, a long, long time. Just for you. Come! Come join the Carnival!"

"What . . . ? Uh . . . ? How . . . ?" I stammered like some pole-axed yokum. *Me,* Fred, old Supercharged Spence.

She laughed, reached up, curled her hands around my neck and kissed me. Her mouth was warm and open, and the taste of her breath made me forget everything. I moved my body against her, asking *the* question, and she answered me with a counter-pressure that was more than a compliance, more certain than an open invitation.

She snaked her hands down my neck, over my shoulders, across my chest, and took both my hands in hers. She nodded toward the choked, swirling streets. "Come on," she said. "The best night of your life is waiting for you, and the darkness is just beginning."

"How long . . . ? How long does all this go on?" I somehow managed to say.

She laughed, a long, wild laugh that made me burn and made me shiver. "Forever!" she cried maniacally. "For you, this can be the night that lasts forever!"

And before I could say a word, before I could tell whether I was eager or afraid, she tugged at my hands, and we were off into the carnivaling city together.

It was dusk—I don't know what time it was by the revolution of Mindalla, but in that impossible city it was a winey, misty, red dusk, and dusk it remained as long as I stayed there, a heady night that always seemed about to fall.

She led me through the streets, through the laughing, packed streets, past knots of humans and 'Bodas and Dreers, open stands offering food and wine and drugs from all over the galaxy, and finally into . . . a house? a room? a place?

A great round hall, the "walls" a circle of marble columns, past which I caught glimpses of other halls and rooms and passageways beyond, that seemed to go on and on and on, a labyrinth of rooms and hallways packed with people and beings and tables bearing food and drink, an endless, continuous party that wound through the hall and the rooms beyond and perhaps the entire city, without limits, without end.

We ate from tables piled with the delicacies of scores of cultures, dozens of worlds; caviar, mulgish, roast boar, sharshu-ding, pilaf, cheeses, cakes, breads, majoun. . . . And strangely, my hunger, though never sharp, lasted through it all, through a feast that seemed to go on for hours.

We drifted from crowded room to packed courtyard. A dark chamber where naked women danced to the pounding beat of African drums. . . . An open court by the golden river where we sat on white sands, inhaling *moutar* from Topaz, and watched the Golden Ones do their insidious Water Dance. . . . A neon-lit room where weirdly dressed kids danced to the music of an ancient Terran rock band. . . .

The amorphous building seemed to be the city itself, and the city was one wild carnival of food and music and dancing, swirling, laughing, completely carrying me away. It seemed that I had but to think of something—a certain food, a wine I remembered, a music I had heard, and it was *there*, anything I ever wanted, ever could want.

And when the time came when there was only *one* more thing I wanted, we turned a corner, stepped through a doorway, and . . .

We were suddenly alone. We were floating in a dark chamber, floating in nothing at all. A velvet, buoying nothing, softer somehow than free-fall itself. She threw aside her robes, and all at once her body seemed to glow with a warm, golden light. She plucked at my clothes, and then I was naked too, and my body was glowing from within like hers.

When we made love, it seemed as if we were alone in the whole universe, the light of our bodies the only light there was. She was perfect . . . and I was *better*. You know me, Fred, so you know what I mean when I say it was the best I had ever had, and the best I had ever been. It made me forget every woman I had ever known.

And afterward I wasn't tired at all—I was full of vitamins and ready for another night of partying. So we laughed and kissed, and it was back to that endless, fantastic party.

And this time around, I felt that the eyes of every woman there were on me. Ever have that feeling? I suppose *you* never have, Fred. But I felt like the cock of the walk; I somehow knew that any woman there I wanted would be mine, and glad to be of service. But it only made me eager for another go at the chick with the white, white skin and the green hair. I somehow knew that I would have plenty of time to sample the rest of them, all the time in the world. . . .

So the spirit moved me again, and we were alone again. We swam nude in a pool of golden water heated to blood-heat under a huge silver moon (on moonless Mindalla), and then we stretched out on a lawn of bright green grass while a warm, perfumed breeze swiftly dried our bodies. I reached out, touched one perfect breast. . . .

"Spence . . ." she moaned.

It brought me up short. I suddenly went cold. I never told her my name. That one impossibility somehow reminded me that I was in the middle of a swamp, a swamp where there *was* no city, where . . . I was afraid, furious and afraid.

I pulled my hand away. "Who are you?" I snapped. "What is—"

She leaned toward me, kissed me, and the question seemed stupid, trivial. . . .

But something in me was still fighting it. I shoved her away. "What the hell is all this? What's going on here?"

She looked at me, a strange, pleading look in her eyes. She laughed a wicked, sensual laugh. "Do you *really* have to know?" she sighed.

But I wasn't buying. *Something* was being done to me, and I had to know what.

"Tell me!" I roared. "Tell me or—"

She began to cry, wilt, whimper. I felt like a heartless monster. "If you insist . . ." she said, "I've got to tell you. But don't insist—take my word for it, Spence, you won't like what you hear. What do you care what we are, where you are? Look around you, smell the air, hear the music, touch my body. Do you want to lose all this? Can any place be like this for you again? Will you ever have another night like this, ever, ever?"

I felt a terrible, aching sadness. I knew she was right, knew that this moment, right now, this night and no other, past or future, was the best I could ever know. I was a spacer with less than two years left on my Papers, and suddenly I felt like an old, old man—from this moment the rest of my life could only be a long, gray downhill slide to nothingness.

"It doesn't have to be," she said, as if reading my mind. "This moment, this night, this place, this Carnival, never has to end. Not for you. Forever, Spence. It can last forever, and forever is a long, long time. . . ."

"Tell me!" I screamed, shaking her shoulders, driven by some savage compulsion, perhaps the knowledge that I was being offered something that in another moment I would be powerless to resist.

Suddenly, a terrible pain sheered through my head, and the city, the pool, *her,* flickered for a moment and were gone.

I was lying on the moist black swamp earth. I was dressed. My clothes were clammy, my stomach ached with hunger. It was night.

And I was alone.

Then I heard a voice in my mind, a cold, chitinous voice like a million crabs clicking their claws in my head. "A billion years," the voice said, and the very sound, the sandpaper feel of it, filled me with dread. "A billion years is a long time to be alone, unused, discarded like a broken toy."

"Who . . . What are you? Her . . . ? The city . . . ?"

"You . . ." the voice in my mind rasped. "Mostly you, a little of me. I looked into your mind, read your memories, your desires, things you didn't even know yourself, and I gave it to you. What you wanted, what you *really* wanted. It was easy. That's what I was . . . *made* for doing. A billion years ago."

"All an illusion?" I stammered. "Just a reflection of my dreams?"

The voice laughed, a hideous, crawling mental sound that set every nerve in my body screaming. "You underestimate the subtlety of the Masters," the voice said. "Those you call the Race With No Name. No mere wish-fulfillment for them. Every world in this galaxy was theirs, but it was not enough for *them.* They craved new worlds, subjective worlds, worlds that lived and breathed and reflected their private whims, but worlds that were still apart from their minds, worlds that held surprises for their dirty, jaded minds. None of them mere dreams, but none of them real."

"But you . . . you're real! You're talking to me now!"

"I'm real," the voice said, words dripping sour acid. "You would call me an . . . *artifact.* They created me out of metal and force . . . and things you could never understand. They gave me the power to read the innermost thoughts and desires of all sentient beings, the power to spin dreams, beautiful dreams without end. A toy, just a toy. But they wanted more, they wanted passion. So they made me sentient, a living, caring thing, a thing with a will and only one motivation—the passion to please a sentient being, any sentient being. And then, a billion years ago, they left for I know not where, and they left me here to rot, flung aside when they no longer were amused by their toy. They left me here to rot and suffer and yearn to please a sentient being. For a billion years, a billion empty years till humans came to this planet."

I shivered in the warm night, felt monstrous things staring at me from out of the black, black night, from out of the unthinkable, distant past.

"But . . . you're not a woman?" I said.

"I can give you every woman you could ever learn to want," the voice said.

"I . . . I want to see you . . ." I stammered.

"I cannot disobey the order of a sentient being," the voice said. "No matter how much I want to. . . ."

There was a movement in the trees, and I saw a dark shape, a slithering, metallic thing, a lump of darkness blacker than the night . . . A wet sound . . . A cold, cold wind across my face, a vortex of . . . of something my eyes could not focus on. I felt myself falling into a black, black pool, eaten alive by green squamous things. . . .

I screamed and screamed and screamed.

And all at once I was standing in the middle of the diamond bridge, and *she* was standing before me.

"I can't keep you from going," she said. She kissed me and gestured toward the great emerald spires, the Carnival that went on and on and on . . .

"All yours, Spence," she said. "Your own private heaven. A universe all for you, a universe that was made for you. Think of it—being made love to by a whole universe. A night of pleasure that never ends. Forever, Spence, a special kind of forever."

"What . . . what kind of forever?"

She laughed, touched me lightly on the lips. "What does it matter?" she said. "A second, an hour, a day, a year, a billion years. If it *seems* like forever, it *is* forever, isn't it, Spence? And I can make it seem like forever. You know I can. I can't keep you from going . . . but can *you* keep you from coming back?"

Then she was gone, and the city was gone, and I was alone in the silence of the Swamp. I stumbled forward a few steps, and my feet clattered against something in the dark, something hard and round. I reached down, touched it, and pulled my hand back.

It was a skull. A human skull. I remembered the Mindallan spacer, and I felt the gnawing hunger in my guts, and I remembered that in the city I had eaten and eaten and eaten . . .

What kind of forever?

Now you know why I'm writing to you, Fred. Soon my Papers will expire, and I'll have to pick one lousy planet out of a whole galaxy on which to spend the rest of my life . . . Please, Fred, talk me out of it! Say something, anything, that will make it seem wrong. But make it good, brother mine, make it good. Say something, anything, that will keep me from going back to Mindalla.

Spence

Sulwen's Planet

by Jack Vance

1

Professor Jason Gench, Professor Victor Kosmin, Dr. Lawrence Drewe, and twenty-four others of equal note filed from the spaceship, to contemplate the scene on Sulwen Plain below. The wondering mutters dwindled to silence; a hollow facetiousness met no response. Professor Gench glanced sidelong toward Professor Kosmin, to encounter Professor Kosmin's bland stare. Gench jerked his gaze away.

Boorish bumbling camel, thought Gench.

Piffling little jackanapes, thought Kosmin.

Each wished the other twelve hundred and four light-years distant: which is to say, back on Earth. Or twelve hundred and five light-years.

The first man on Sulwen Plain had been James Sulwen, an embittered Irish Nationalist turned space-wanderer. In his memoirs Sulwen wrote: "To say I was startled, awed, dumfounded, is like saying the ocean is wet. Oh, but it's a lonesome place, so far away, so dim and cold, the more so for the mystery. I stayed there three days and two nights, taking pictures, wondering about the history, all the histories of the universe. What had happened so long ago? What had brought these strange folk here to die? I became haunted; I had to leave . . ."

Sulwen returned to Earth with his photographs. His discovery was hailed as "the single most important event in human history." Public interest reached a level of dizzy excitement; here was cosmic drama at its most vivid: mystery, tragedy, cataclysm.

In such a perfervid atmosphere the "Sulwen Planet Survey Commission" was nominated, and instructed to perform a brief investigation upon which a full-scale program of research could be based. No one thought to point out that the function of Professor Victor Kosmin, in the field of comparative linguistics, and that of Professor Jason Gench, a philologist, overlapped. The Director of the commission was Dr. Lawrence Drewe, Fellow of Mathematical Philosophy at Vidmar Institute: a mild wry gentleman, superficially inadequate to the job of controlling the personalities of the other members of the commission.

Accompanied by four supply transports with men, materials, and machinery for the construction of a permanent base, the commission departed Earth.

2

Sulwen had understated the desolation of Sulwen's Plain. A dwarf white sun cast a wan glare double, or possibly triple, the intensity of full moonlight. Basalt crags rimmed the plain to north and east. A mile from the base of the crags was the first of the seven wrecked spaceships: a collapsed cylinder of black-and-white metal two hundred and forty feet long, a hundred and two feet in diameter. There were five such hulks. In and out of the ships, perfectly preserved in the scant atmosphere of frigid nitrogen, were the corpses of a squat pallid race, something under human size, with four arms, each terminating in two fingers.

The remaining two ships, three times the length and twice the diameter of the black-and-white ships, had been conceived and constructed on a larger, more flamboyant, scale. Big Purple, as it came to be known, was undamaged except for a gash down the length of its dorsal surface. Big Blue had crashed nose-first to the planet and stood in an attitude of precarious equilibrium, seemingly ready to topple at a touch. The design of Big Purple and Big Blue was eccentric, refined, and captious, implying esthetic intent or some analogous quality. These ships were manned by tall slender blue-black creatures with many-horned heads and delicate pinched faces half-concealed behind tufts of hair. They became known as Wasps and their enemies, the pale creatures, were labeled Sea Cows, though in neither case was the metaphor particularly apt.

Sulwen's Plain had been the site of a terrible battle between two spacefaring races: so much was clear. Three questions occurred simultaneously to each of the commissioners:

Where did these peoples originate?

How long ago had the battle occurred?

How did the technology of the Wasps and Sea Cows compare with that of Earth?

There was no immediate answer to the first question. Sulwen's Star controlled no other planets.

As to the time of the battle, a first estimate, derived from the deposition of meteoric dust, suggested a figure of fifty thousand years. More accurate determinations ultimately put the time at sixty-two thousand years.

The third question was more difficult to answer. In some cases Wasp, Sea Cow, and man had come by different routes to similar ends. In other cases, no comparison was possible.

There was endless speculation as to the course of the battle. The most popular theory envisioned the Sea Cow ships sweeping down upon Sulwen's Plain to find Big Blue and Big Purple at rest. Big Blue had lifted perhaps half a mile, only to be crippled and plunge nose-first to the surface. Big Purple, with a mortal gash down the back, apparently had never left the ground. Perhaps other ships had been present; there was no way of knowing. By one agency or another five Sea Cow ships had been destroyed.

3

The ships from Earth landed on a rise to the southeast of the battlefield, where James Sulwen originally had put down. The commissioners, debarking in their out-suits, walked out to the nearest Sea Cow ship: Sea Cow D, as it became known. Sulwen's Star hung low to the horizon, casting a stark pallid light. Long black shadows lay across the putty-colored plain.

The commissioners studied the ruptured ship, inspected the twisted Sea Cow corpses, then Sulwen's Star dropped below the horizon. Instant darkness came to the plain, and the commissioners, looking often over their shoulders, returned to their own ship.

After the evening meal, Director Drewe addressed the group: "This is a preliminary survey. I reiterate because we are scientists: we want to know! We are not so much interested in planning research as in the research itself. Well—we must practice restraint. For most of you, these wrecks will occupy many years to come. I myself, alas! am a formalist, a mathematical theorist, and as such will be denied such an opportunity. Well, then, my personal problems aside: Temporarily we must resign ourselves to ignorance. The mystery will remain a mystery, unless Professor Gench or Professor Kosmin instantly is able to read one of the languages." Here Drewe chuckled; he had intended the remark jocularly. Noticing the quick, suspicious glance exchanged by Gench and Kosmin, he decided that the remark had not been tactful. "For a day or two I suggest a casual inspection of the project, to orient ourselves. There is no pressure on us; we will achieve more if we relax, and try to achieve a wide-angle view of the situation. And by all means, everyone be careful of the big blue ship. It looks as if it might topple at a breath!"

Professor Gench smiled bitterly. He was thin as a shrike, with a gaunt crooked face, a crag of a forehead, a black angry gaze. "No pressure on us," he thought. "What a joke!"

"Relax!" thought Kosmin, with a sardonic twitch of the lips. "With that preposterous Gench underfoot? Pah!" In contrast to Gench, Kosmin was massive, almost portly, with a big pale face, a tuft of yellow hair. His cheekbones were heavy, his forehead narrow and back-sloping. He made no effort to project an ingratiating personality; no more so did Gench. Of the two, Gench was perhaps the more gregarious, but his approach to any situation, social or professional, tended to be sharp and doctrinaire.

"I will perform some quick and brilliant exposition," Gench decided. "I must put Kosmin in his place."

"One man eventually will direct the linguistics program," mused Kosmin. "Who but a comparative linguist?"

Drewe concluded his remarks. "I need hardly urge all to

caution. Be careful of your footing; do not venture into closed areas. You naturally will be wearing out-suits; check your regenerators and energy levels before leaving the ship; keep your communications channels open at all times. Another matter: let us try to disturb conditions as little as possible. This is a monumental job, there is no point rushing forth, worrying at it like a dog with a rag. Well, then: a good night's rest and tomorrow, have at it!"

4

The commissioners stepped out upon the dreary surface of the plain, approached the wrecked ships. The closest at hand was Sea Cow D, a black-and-white vessel, battered, broken, littered with pale corpses. The metallurgists touched analyzers to various sections of hull and machinery reading off alloy compositions; the biologists went to examine the corpses; the physicists and technicians peered into the engine compartments, marveling at the engineering of an alien race. Gench, walking under the hulk, found a strip of white fiber, covered with rows of queer smears. As he lifted it, the fiber, brittle from cold and age, fell to pieces.

Kosmin, noticing, shook his head critically. "Precisely what you must not do!" he told Gench. "A valuable piece of information is lost forever."

Gench drew his lips back across his teeth. "So much is self-evident. Since the basic responsibility is mine, you need not trouble yourself with doubts or anxieties."

Kosmin ignored Gench's remarks as if he had never spoken. "In the future, please do not move or disturb an important item without consulting me."

Gench turned a withering glare upon his ponderous colleague. "As I interpret the scope of your work, you are to compare the languages after I have deciphered them. You are thus happily able to indulge your curiosity without incurring any immediate responsibility."

Kosmin did not trouble to refute Gench's proposition. "Please disturb no further data. You have carelessly destroyed an artifact. Consult me before you touch anything." And he moved off across the plain toward Big Purple.

Gench, hissing between his teeth, hesitated, then hastened

in pursuit. Left to his own devices, Kosmin was capable of any excess. Gench told himself, "Two can play that game!"

Most of the group now stood about Big Purple, which, enormous and almost undamaged, dominated Sulwen's Plain. The hull was a rough-textured lavender substance striped with four horizontal bands of corroded metal: apparently a component of the drive-system. Only a powdering of dust and crystals of frozen gas gave an intimation of its great age.

The commissioners walked around the hull, but the ports were sealed. The only access was by the gash along the top surface. A metallurgist found an exterior ladder welded to the hull: he tested the rungs: they seemed sound. While all watched he climbed to the ruptured spine of the ship, gave a jaunty wave of the hand and disappeared.

Gench glanced covertly at Kosmin, who was considering the handholds with lips pursed in distaste. Gench marched forward and climbed the ladder. Kosmin started as if he had been stung. He grimaced, took a step forward, put one of his big legs on the first rung.

Drewe came forward to counsel caution. "Better not risk it, Professor Kosmin; why take chances? I'll have technicians open the port, then we all can enter in safety. We are in no haste, none whatever."

Kosmin thought, "You're in no haste, of course not! And while you dither, that stick-insect in human form walks inside preempting the best of everything!"

This indeed was Gench's intent. Clambering down through the torn hull with his dome-light on, he found himself in a marvelous environment of shapes and colors which could only be characterized, if tritely, by the word "weird."* Certain functional details resembled those of Earth ships, but with odd distortions and differences of proportion that were subtly jarring. "Naturally, and to be expected," Gench told himself. "We alter environment to the convenience of our needs: the length of our tread, the reach of our arms, the

---

* In Drewe's book *Sulwen's Planet* he remarked: "Color is color and shape is shape; it would seem incorrect to speak of *human* shape and *human* color, and *Wasp* shape and *Wasp* color; but somehow, by some means, the distinction exists. Call me a mystic if you like . . ."

sensitivity of our retinas, many other considerations. And
these other races, likewise . . . Fascinating . . . I suspect that
a man, confined for any length of time in this strange ship,
might become seriously disturbed, if not deranged." With
great interest Gench inspected the Wasp corpses which lay
sprawled along the corridors: blue-black husks, chitinous
surfaces still glossy where dust had not settled. How long
would corpses remain unaltered, Gench wondered. Forever?
Why not? At 100° K, in an inert atmosphere, it was difficult
to imagine changes occurring except those stimulated by cosmic rays . . . But to work. No time now for speculation! He
had stolen a march on the torpid Kosmin, and he meant to
make the most of it.

One encouraging matter: there was no lack of writing. Everywhere were signs, plaques, notices in angular interweaving
lines which at first glance offered no hope of decipherment.
Gench was pleased rather than otherwise. The task would be
challenging, but with the aid of computers, pattern-recogniz-
ing devices, keys, and correlations derived from a study of the
context in which the symbols occurred (here indeed lay the
decipherer's basic contribution to the process) the language
eventually would be elucidated. Another matter: aboard a
ship of this size there might well exist not only a library, but
rosters, inventories, service manuals pertaining to the various
mechanisms: a wealth of material! And Gench saw his problem to be, not the decipherment, but the presence of Professor
Kosmin.

Gench shook his head fretfully. A damnable nuisance! He
must have a word with Director Drewe. Kosmin perhaps
could be assigned to another task: indexing material to be
transhipped to Earth, something of the sort.

Gench proceeded through the corridors and levels of Big
Purple, trying to locate either a central repository of written
materials, or, failing this, the control center. But the ship's
architecture was not instantly comprehensible and Gench was
initially unsuccessful. Wandering back and forth, he found
himself in what appeared to be a storage hold, stacked with
cases and cartons, then, descending a ramp, he came to the
base level and an entry foyer. The port had been forced; commissioners and technicians were passing in and out. Gench
halted in disgust, then returned the way he had come:

through the storage hold, along corridors, up and down ramps. He began meeting other members of the commission, and hurried his steps to such an extent that his colleagues turned to look after him in surprise. At last he came to the control room, though it bore no resemblance to the corresponding office of any Earth ship, and in fact Gench had passed through before without recognizing its function.

Professor Kosmin, already on hand, glanced around at Gench, then resumed the examination of what appeared to be a large book.

Gench marched indignantly forward. "Professor Kosmin, I prefer that you do not disturb the source materials, or move them, as the context in which they are found may be important."

Kosmin gave Gench a mild glance and returned to his scrutiny of the book.

"Please be extremely careful," said Professor Gench. "If any materials are damaged through mishandling—well, they are irreplaceable." Gench stepped forward. Kosmin moved slightly, but somehow contrived to thrust his ample haunch into Gench, and thus barred his way.

Gench glared at his colleague's back, then turned and departed the chamber.

He sought out Director Drewe. "Director, may I have a word with you?"

"Certainly."

"I fear that my investigations, and indeed the success of the entire translation program, are being compromised by the conduct of Professor Kosmin, who insists upon intruding into my scope of operation. I am sorry to trouble you with a complaint of this sort, but I feel that a decisive act now on your part will enormously facilitate my work."

Director Drewe sighed. "Professor Kosmin has taken a similar position. Something must be done. Where is he now?"

"In the control chamber, thumbing through an absolutely vital element of the investigation, as if it were a discarded magazine."

Drewe and Gench walked toward the control chamber. Gench said, "I suggest that you use Professor Kosmin in some administrative capacity: logging, indexing, compilation, or the like, until the translation program is sufficiently advanced that he may employ his specialized talents. As of now—ha, ha!—there are no languages for him to compare!"

Drewe made no comment. In the control room they found Kosmin still absorbed in the book.

"What have we here?" inquired Drewe.

"Hmm. Umph . . . A highly important find. It appears to be—I may be over-optimistic—a dictionary, a word-book, a correspondence between the languages of the two races."

"If this is the case," declared Gench, "I had better take charge of it at once."

Drewe heaved a deep sigh. "Gentlemen, temporarily, at any rate, we must arrange a division of function so that neither you, Professor Kosmin, nor you, Professor Gench, are hampered. There are two races here, two languages. Professor Kosmin, which of the two interests you the more profoundly?"

"That is difficult to say," rumbled Kosmin. "I am not yet acquainted with either."

"What about you, Professor Gench?"

With his eyes fixed on the book, Gench said, "My first emphasis will be upon the records of this ship, though naturally, when the inquiry is expanded and I assemble a staff, I will devote equal effort to the other ships."

"Bah!" declared Kosmin, with as much emphasis as he ever permitted himself. "I will work first at this ship," he told Drewe. "It is more convenient. On the other hand, I would wish to insure that source material elsewhere is handled competently. I have already reported the loss of one irreplaceable record."

Drewe nodded. "It seems that there is no possibility of agreement, let alone cooperation. Very well." He picked up a small metal disk. "We will consider this a coin. This side with the two nicks we will call heads. The other will be tails. Professor Gench, be so good as to call heads or tails while the disk is in the air. If you call correctly, you may concentrate your research on the two large ships."

He tossed the disk.

"Heads," called Gench.

"The coin is tails," said Drewe. "Professor Gench, you will survey the five black-and-white ships. Professor Kosmin, your responsibility will be the two larger ships. This seems a fair division of effort, and neither will inconvenience the other."

Kosmin made a guttural sound. Gench scowled and bit his lip. Neither was satisfied with the decision. With each familiar with only half of the program, a third man might be appointed to supervise and coordinate the labors of both.

Drewe said, "You both must remember that this is a survey expedition. What is required are suggestions as to how the research should be performed, not the research itself."

Kosmin turned to examine the book he had found. Gench threw his hands in the air and strode furiously away.

5

The season seemed to be summer. Sulwen's Star, a glittering sequin, rose far to the southeast, slanted up into the northern sky, slanted back down into the southwest, and black shadows shifted in consonance around the wrecked hulks. The construction crews erected a pair of polyhedric bubbles and the commission moved into more comfortable quarters.

On the fourth evening, as Sulwen's Star touched the edge of the plain, Drewe called his fellow-commissioners together.

"By now," he said, "I think we all have come to grips with the situation. I myself have done little but wander here and there. In fact, I fear I am but excess baggage on the expedition. Well—as I have said before—enough of my personal hopes and fears. What have we learned? There seems a consensus that both races were technically more advanced than ourselves, though this may only be an intuition, a guess. As to their relative level—who knows? But let us have an inventory, an assessment of our mutual findings."

The physicists expressed astonishment at the radically different solutions to the problem of space-drive reached by the three races: man, Sea Cow, and Wasp. The chemist speculated as to the probable atmosphere breathed by Wasp and Sea Cow, and commented upon some of the new compounds they had encountered aboard the ships. The engineers were somewhat nonplussed, having noticed unorthodox systems not readily susceptible to analysis which could not be dismissed out of hand as the result of incompetence. The biochemists could provide no immediate insight into the metabolic processes of either Wasp or Sea Cow.

Drewe called for an opinion on the languages, and the possibility of translation. Professor Gench rose to his feet, cleared his throat, only to hear the hated voice of Professor Kosmin issuing from another quarter of the room. "As of yet," said Kosmin, "I have given little attention to the Sea Cow language or system of writing. The Wasps, so I have learned from Professor Hideman and Doctor Miller, lack vocal cords, or equivalent organs. They seem to have produced sound by a scraping of certain bony parts behind a resonating membrane. Their conversation, it has been suggested, sounded like a cheap violin played by an idiot child." And Kosmin gave one of his rare oily chuckles. "The writing corresponds to this 'speech' much as human writing corresponds to human speech. In other words, a vibrating, fluctuating sound is transcribed by a vibrating, fluctuating line: a difficult language to decipher. Naturally, not impossible. I have made one very important find: a compendium or dictionary of Sea Cow pictographs referred to their equivalent in the Wasp written system—a proof, incidentally, that the work of translating both languages must be entrusted to a single agency, and I will formulate a scheme to this end. I welcome the help of all of you; if anyone notices a clear-cut correspondence between symbol and idea, please call it to my attention. I have entrusted to Professor Gench the first cursory examination of the Sea Cow ships, but as of yet I have not checked through his findings." Kosmin continued a few minutes longer, then Drewe called on Professor Gench for his report. Gench leaped to his feet, lips twitching. He spoke with great care. "The program Professor Kosmin mentions is naturally standard procedure. Professor Kosmin, a comparator of known languages, may well be excused for ignorance of deciphering techniques. With two such difficult languages no one need feel shame—ha, ha!—for working beyond his depth. The dictionary mentioned by Professor Kosmin is a valuable item indeed and I suggest that Director Drewe put it into safe custody or entrust it into my care. We cannot risk its abuse by untrained amateurs and dilettantes. I am pressing my search for a similar compendium aboard the Sea Cow ships.

"I would like to announce a small but significant accomplishment. I have established the Sea Cow numerical system and it is much like our own. An unbroken black rectangle is zero. A single bar is one. A cross-bar is two. An inverted *u*, conventionalized perhaps from a triangle, is three. A digit resembling our own two is the Sea Cow four. And so on. Perhaps Professor Kosmin has established the Wasp numeration?"

Kosmin, who had been listening without expression, said, "I have been busy with the work for which I was appointed: the formation and supervision of a decipherment program. Numbers at the moment are no great matter."

"I will look over your formulations," said Gench. "If any aspects seem well conceived I will include them in the master program I am preparing. Here I wish to utter a testimonial to Professor Kosmin. He was urged into the commission against his better judgment, he was assigned a task for which he had no training; nonetheless he has uncomplainingly done his best, even though he is anxious to return to Earth and the work he so generously interrupted in our behalf." And Gench, with a grin and bob of the head, bowed toward Kosmin. From the other members of the commission came a spatter of dubious applause.

Kosmin rose ponderously to his feet. "Thank you, Professor Gench." He reflected a moment. "I have not heard any report on the condition of Big Blue. It seems precariously balanced, but on the other hand it has remained in stasis for thousands of years. I wonder if there has been any decision as to the feasibility of boarding this ship?" He peered toward the engineers.

Director Drewe responded: "I don't think there has been any definite verdict here. For the present I think we had better stand clear of it."

"Unfortunate," said Kosmin. "It appears that the damage suffered by Big Purple destroyed that chamber which served as a repository of written materials. The corresponding location of Big Blue by some freak is quite undamaged, and I am anxious to investigate."

Gench sat kneading his long chin.

"In due course, in due course," said Drewe. "Yes, Professor Gench?"

Gench frowned down at his hands. He spoke slowly, "It may interest the commission to learn that aboard Sea Cow B, the ship north of Big Purple, I have located just such a repository of Sea Cow documents, though I haven't checked the contents yet. This repository is in Room Eleven on the second deck from ground level and seems to be the only such repository undamaged."

"Interesting news," said Drewe, squinting sidelong toward Gench. "Interesting indeed. Well, then, to the drive technicians: what, offhand, do you make of the Wasp and Sea Cow space-drives, vis-à-vis each other and our own?"

The meeting lasted another hour. Director Drewe made a final announcement. "Our primary goal has almost been achieved, and unless there is a pressing reason to the contrary, I think that we will start back to Earth in two days. Kindly base your thinking upon this timetable."

6

The following morning Professor Gench continued his investigations about Sea Cow B. At lunch he appeared highly excited. "I believe I have located a Wasp-Sea Cow compendium in Room Eleven of Sea Cow B! An amazing document! This afternoon I must check Sea Cow E for a similar storeroom."

Professor Kosmin, sitting two tables distant, lowered his head over his plate.

7

Gench seemed somewhat nervous, and his fingers trembled as he zipped himself into his out-suit. He stepped out upon the plain. Directly overhead glittered Sulwen's Star: The wrecked ships stood like models, without human reality or relevance.

Sea Cow E lay a mile to the south. Gench marched stiffly across the plain, from time to time glancing back at other personnel, unidentifiable in out-suits. His course took him past Big Blue and he veered so as to pass close under the great broken ship. He turned another quick glance over his shoulder: no one in his field of vision. He glanced up at the precariously balanced hulk. "Safe? Safe as jelly-bread." He stepped through a gap in the hull, into a picturesque tangle of girders, plates, membranes, and fibers.

Professor Kosmin, watching Gench veer toward Big Blue, nodded: three jerks of the massive head. "Well, then. Now we shall see, we shall see." He walked north toward Sea Cow B, and presently stood by the crushed hull. "The entrance? Yes

. . . To the second deck then . . . Surprising architecture. What peculiar coloring . . . Hmm. Room Eleven. The numerals are clear enough. This is the one, the single bar. And here the two." Kosmin proceeded along the corridor. "Six . . . seven . . . Strange. Ten. Where is eight and nine? Well, no matter. Unlucky numbers perhaps. Here is ten and here eleven. Aha." Kosmin pushed aside the panel and entered Chamber Eleven.

8

Sulwen's Star slanted down to the gray horizon and past; darkness came instantly to the plain. Neither Gench nor Kosmin appeared for the evening meal. The steward called Director Drewe's attention to the fact.

Drewe considered the two empty seats. "I suppose we must send out to find them. Professor Gench will no doubt be exploring Big Blue. I presume we will find Professor Kosmin hard at work in Sea Cow B."

9

Professor Gench had suffered a broken collarbone, contusions, and shock from the blow of the heavy beam which Professor Kosmin—so Gench claimed—had arranged to fall upon whoever might enter Big Blue's control cabin.

"Not so!" boomed Professor Kosmin, both of whose legs had been broken as a result of his fall through the floor of Chamber Eleven on the second deck of Sea Cow B. "You were warned expressly not to set foot in Big Blue. How could I set a trap in a place you were forbidden to visit? What of the detestable pitfall by which you hoped to kill me? Aha, but I am too strong for you! I caught the floor and broke my fall! I survived your worst!"

"You survive your own stupidity," sneered Gench. "Sea Cows, with two fingers on each of four arms, use base eight in their enumerations. You went into Chamber Nine, not Chamber Eleven. A person as obtuse and as muderous as yourself has no place in the field of science! I am lucky to be alive!"

"Were my legs sound I would tread upon you for the roach you are!" shouted Professor Kosmin.

Director Drewe intervened. "Gentlemen, calm yourselves. Reproaches are futile; remorse is more appropriate. you must realize that neither of you will head the decipherment program."

"Indeed? And why not?" snorted Gench.

"Under the circumstances I fear that I can recommend neither of you."

"Then who will be appointed?" demanded Kosmin. "The field is not crowded with able men."

Drewe shrugged. "As a mathematician, I may say that deciphering appeals to me as a fascinating exercise in logic. I might be persuaded to accept the post myself. To be candid, it is probably my only chance for continued association with the project." Director Drewe bowed politely and left the room.

Professor Gench and Professor Kosmin were silent for several minutes. Then Gench said, "Peculiar. Very peculiar indeed. I arranged no pitfall in Chamber Nine. I admit I had noted that the panel could be opened from one direction only, from the corridor . . . A person venturing into Chamber Nine might find himself in a humiliating position . . . Strange."

"Hmm," rumbled Kosmin. "Strange indeed . . ."

There was another period of silence as the two men reflected. Then Kosmin said, "Of course I am not altogether innocent. I conceived that if you ventured into Big Blue against orders you would incur a reprimand. I propped up no beam."

"Most peculiar," said Professor Gench. "A puzzling situation . . . A possibility suggests itself—"

"Yes?"

"Why kill us?"

"To the mathematical mind the most elegant solution is the simplest," reflected Professor Kosmin.

"A canceling of the unknowns," mused Professor Gench.

A Merriam-Webster
REG U S PAT OFF

THE LEADING NAME IN DICTIONARIES SINCE 1847

REG U S PAT OFF

The New
MERRIAM-WEBSTER
POCKET
DICTIONARY

This 640 page pocket-size dictionary has been specially prepared for general use by the recognized leading dictionary makers.

MORE THAN 42,000 VOCABULARY ENTRIES

GUIDES TO SPELLING AND PRONUNCIATION

SELECTED ETYMOLOGIES GIVING PRECISE WORD HISTORIES

SYNONYMS

COMMONLY USED ABBREVIATIONS

FOREIGN WORDS AND PHRASES

POPULATION FIGURES FOR THE UNITED STATES AND CANADA

75320 / 75¢